WILD STALLIONS

THE HONEYWELLS OF KENTUCKY, BOOK 1

VANESSA GRAY BARTAL

DRY CREEK PRESS

The Honeywells were famous, and not because they had more money than Zeus. Lots of horse families in the Lexington area had money. No, the family was famous for a different reason--notorious, really--because of their children.

First of all there were six of them, five boys and a girl. Their mother had initially wanted twelve children and, like her favorite movie *Seven Brides for Seven Brothers*, decided to name them alphabetically. The oldest, Adam, died at birth. Between the two youngest boys, Everett and Grant, there had been a stillborn baby. He was given an *F* name that no one but his parents knew. Then there was another miscarriage between Grant and his sister, Ivy. This baby was named with an *H*.

The girl, Ivy, wasn't the problem. Everyone who had met her or even seen her knew right away she was nothing like her brothers. Sweet, quiet, and most of all blond, she stuck out like a sore thumb when the group was together. Despite her beauty, most people figured she would never get married because the man who married her would also have to take on her hooligan brothers. But then she went away and married a man in Montana, about as far from her brothers as she could get while still remaining in the United States. People around town, who were usually born and buried within a mile of everyone they knew, didn't begrudge the youngest Honeywell for getting away. No, they wished her well, glad to see her finally free of her oppressive brothers.

On their own, the brothers were very nice. They were well known for their charitable donations, as well as their random acts of kindness. Unfortunately they were also infamous for their pranks. As a unit they were loud, boisterous, uproarious, and overwhelming. They all looked exactly alike—ridiculously tall with smoldering dark eyes and thick black hair that covered every inch of their bodies. Their masculine handsomeness was as over-the-top as everything else about them. Women found them nice looking but much too terrifying to get close to.

The mystery was how such troublemakers came from such patrician stock. Like the horses they bred, the Honeywells could be traced back generations to the founding of the country and beyond. And nowhere in that history had there ever been such as these. Maybe it was because there were so many of them together that they formed an unbreakable unit. Whatever the reason, and although no one would speak it out loud, most people in town were scared witless at the sight of them. Some people thought they preferred it that way. Some people were wrong.

The Honeywell brothers had no idea the way people perceived them because they had no idea their behavior was anything abnormal. They did what they wanted and what made them laugh, not realizing that sometimes they were laughing at the expense of others. As they neared their thirties and began to mature out of their boyish ways, they were frustrated that no one seemed willing to let their pasts go, but unsure how to change the perception they had created. This problem was made worse by the fact that, to them, settling down meant no more streaking through the town on national holidays.

They had no idea what it took to love a woman and be loved in return, something each of them wanted but would never admit. But very soon that was all about to change because the Honeywells were about to fall like dominoes and, as everyone knew, they did nothing conventionally or halfheartedly—love being no exception.

CHAPTER 1

*B*rent Honeywell was glad to be alone. Not that he begrudged having so many siblings, because he didn't. He enjoyed his brothers and his little sister, probably more than the average seventeen year old. But every once in a while, it was nice to enjoy some solitude. Especially now that his next youngest brother, Corliss, had recently procured his driver's license. Their parents stubbornly refused to buy more than one truck, stating the brothers would have to learn to share.

For an entire year until Corliss turned sixteen, Brent had enjoyed the novelty of being the only one able to drive—a new experience because, being from such a large family, he'd learned early to share everything. Now the dream was over, and he had to give up control of his precious truck. At least he had gotten to drive it when it was brand new. By the time Ivy learned to drive, the truck would be a jalopy, if they ever let her drive, which was doubtful. As the only girl, Ivy needed to be protected. The sooner she learned that and stopped struggling, the better off they all would be.

Being off work was another thing that made this day special. He didn't begrudge work, either. He loved working his family's horse farm, loved every aspect of it, but sometimes change was nice. Being alone and away from work was so different from his everyday life that he almost didn't know what to do with himself. Almost. In the end, he decided to simply get in the truck and drive, enjoying his last bit of freedom while it lasted. Summer was winding down soon. Since he was seventeen and had graduated high school, the end of summer didn't have as much meaning for him, but he still felt the same sense of longing as the days waned.

Maybe it was because he secretly wanted to go to college this year like his peers. Taking a gap year had seemed like a good idea at the time, but now he wasn't so sure. What if he felt old when he finally went to school next year?

His thoughts rambled and he let them, glad for the silence that allowed him to think for once. He was on the highway, the cruise control set, and the radio tuned to his favorite station. It was a perfect day, and nothing could go wrong.

But almost as soon as he hatched the thought, something went horribly, terribly wrong. A car sped through an intersection not more than twenty feet away from him. Brent didn't have a stop sign; the car did but either didn't see or chose to ignore it. Brent stomped the brake until it reached the floor, but it didn't matter. He smashed into the car, t-boning the driver's side. His seatbelt jerked tight with the impact. The two cars, now melded together, skidded for at least a hundred feet before coming to a halt. Brent blinked, dazed. His ears rang and his shoulder hurt, but he didn't think he was seriously injured. The other car, though…

He patted his pockets, frantically searching for his fancy new phone. He had bought it to impress girls, but routinely forgot to carry it with him. Today was no exception. He had left it at home. He tried to search the surrounding countryside for houses where he could go for help, but this stretch of highway was deserted.

As soon as his fumbling fingers would allow, he disentangled himself from the truck and hopped down, taking a wobbling step before righting himself. He stood still a minute, waiting for the spinning to stop, and then lurched toward the car.

The driver's side was now a part of his truck; there was no way to get to it and try to open the door. Instead he jogged to the passenger side and flung open the door. A little girl of about five sat in the seat, her brown eyes wide, a phone in her hand.

"Did you call 911?" he asked, amazed when he noted the green light on the phone that indicated a call had been made.

She nodded.

He glanced behind her to the person in the driver's seat. The sight was gruesome. A man, most likely her father, dangled lifelessly from his seatbelt. A large gash in his neck oozed so much blood he had likely bled out before Brent finished unleashing his seatbelt. The girl started to turn toward her father, but Brent didn't want her to look again.

"Do you know who I am?" he asked.

The girl nodded. "You're a Honeywell," she said, her voice shaky.

Despite the situation, Brent smiled at her pluckiness. "I want you to come with me right now." He held out his hand toward her, but she made no move to take it, even though she was staring at it. He noted the widening of her pupils and thought she might be going into shock. *What would I do if this was Ivy?* With thoughts of Ivy in his mind, he reached over the girl, unclasped her seatbelt and lifted her from the car.

He carried her down an embankment several feet away and sat down, cradling her in his arms like a baby. "What's your name?" he asked.

"Haley," she said. Her pupils were getting wider by the second and the blood seemed to be draining from her face, leaving it a deathly shade of white. He squeezed her hand and found it clammy. Frantically, he patted his pocket until he located the sucker he had taken from the bank. He unwrapped it and popped it in her mouth without asking permission. She sucked on it listlessly, staring straight ahead with no expression.

When she started to shake convulsively, he wrapped his arms tightly around her and began to rock. He sang the song he had secretly sung to his sister when she was a baby. Haley rested her head on his chest. Her arms snaked up to cling tightly to his neck, and

Brent cinched his arms around her, willing her bone-rattling trembling to go away.

After what seemed like an eternity, the air was shattered by the scream of several sirens. The first responder on the scene jumped from his cruiser and swore, sure he wouldn't find anyone alive in the tangle of wreckage. When he walked around the mass of twisted metal and only saw one dead man, he scanned the horizon in confusion until he saw two bodies several yards away. Thinking they had been thrown from the vehicles, he went over to them, steeling his emotions for whatever he might find, but he was still shaken by the sight.

One of the Honeywell boys—no one could ever tell them apart—sat on the ground, hugging a small child and rocking back and forth. He sang a quiet lullaby as tears rolled gently down his cheeks. The child, a girl, clung so fiercely to him the officer thought they might need the Jaws of Life to pry her loose. The sight stunned and touched him, mostly because he thought the Honeywell boys incapable of crying. Ashamed of his callous and inappropriate thought, he snapped to attention and began to go to work. However, he couldn't stop his eyes from straying to the Honeywell and the little kid who stayed together until the last possible moment. At last the paramedics tore them apart, loading them into two separate ambulances.

The little girl cried then, for the first time. Her little arms reached for the Honeywell kid as she screamed his name, Brent, over and over. And he reached for her, so forcefully he had to be tied down to the gurney. As the medics were loading him into the squad, the officer caught the same phrase repeated over and over again.

"I'm sorry, Haley, I'm sorry."

CHAPTER 2

Fifteen years later…

"My hand is killing me," Brent said. "It's been a week, and it still hurts."

His brother, Corliss, pointed to his face. "I don't want to hear it. You broke my jaw." At least that's what Brent thought he said; it was difficult to tell because his jaw was wired shut.

"You told me to hit you," Brent said.

Corliss rolled his eyes, not wanting to go over it again. He had meant to wait until he had his new protective boxing gear in place, but since he hadn't specified, Brent went ahead and fulfilled the request as soon as it was made. Corliss couldn't really fault him because he would have done the same thing. Though none of them considered themselves to be violent, all of the brothers liked to hit things. Usually they hit inanimate objects like punching bags or hay bales. But occasionally if the mood struck, they hit each other. Of course, only for fun. They would never actually beat on each other—that would be wrong.

Their three younger brothers, Darcy, Everett, and Grant, sat in the back of the truck, arguing about something. The brothers were always arguing about something. What no one seemed to realize was that they enjoyed arguing with each other. For them, arguing was a form of communication. No one ever got angry in the course of an argument. In fact, Brent couldn't remember the last time one of them had been angry at another. Maybe when they were little and argued over toys, but even then he doubted it. There had never been anything a good fistfight couldn't straighten out.

Tonight was their parents' anniversary, and so the brothers were vacating the house. When they were little, they used to make things for their mother and present them to her as precious treasure. As they aged, they realized what she valued most was a little peace and quiet. So, whenever it was a special occasion, they left the house and gave their parents some time alone. Now they were going out to eat, and they had to drive farther than usual because they had once again been banned from all the restaurants nearby.

Brent didn't understand why they kept getting thrown out of establishments. They ordered a lot of food, true, but they always paid their bill and left a hefty tip. And they weren't messy, either. In an effort not to get thrown out of so many places, they had learned to stack their trays and clean up their trash, thinking that might help, but it hadn't. They still found themselves asked not to return almost every time they ate somewhere. Brent shook his head. He didn't get it. Times were hard. Why didn't places want their business?

His hands tensed as he passed through the intersection. Automatically, his eyes darted right and left as he searched for cars. Maybe if he had looked closer that day, checked and double checked, he would have been able to stop in time. Maybe...

"Brent," Corliss called.

Brent snapped to attention and released his death grip on the steering wheel. He hadn't let the accident stop him from driving, of course. He had driven again the next day. But he remembered, and every time he passed though the intersection there was still that same gut reaction. His brothers knew and never let him become too absorbed in his memories. He eased out a breath and forced himself to relax. There, they were through the intersection and nothing bad had happened. Nothing bad had ever happened since that day. He hadn't even had a fender bender since then, but the memories still lingered.

At last they arrived at the little café outside of their town of Silver Springs. Technically, the family lived in Lexington. Lexington considered Silver Springs a suburb, but Silver Springs did not consider itself a part of Lexington, thank you very much. Lexington was a big city where thugs and drug dealers ran rampant. Silver Springs was a nice family place and would remain that way, which was why they annually voted against being incorporated into Lexington. Lexington made a good case every year, patiently explaining to Silver Springs that they would reap the benefits of being in a city while paying fewer taxes, but every year Silver Springs declined the invitation. They would remain as a small town, and that was that.

The café was under new management and reputed to have good pie. The brothers all shared a sweet tooth and would drive almost anywhere for pie, making the café that was so close to home ideal.

"Let's do our best not to get thrown out of this one," Brent announced to his brothers as soon as they stepped out of the truck.

"What do we ever do to get thrown out of any of the others?" Grant asked.

Brent shrugged. "I have no idea."

They turned as a unit and walked into the small café, overwhelming it with their presence. Was it their imagination that staff and patrons alike came to a sudden halt and stared, anxiety on their faces? The hostess dropped a menu and ducked behind the cash register to pick it up.

"Right this way," she said, her voice shaky with fear. She led them to a table in the center of the restaurant.

"Not this one," Everett said. "That one." He pointed to a booth in the far corner. It only had two seats.

"But…" The hostess began.

"We'll rearrange some things," Darcy told her. He gave her shoulder what he meant to be a gentle pat, but she stumbled forward and grimaced. They got to work and soon had the tables rearranged to their satisfaction. True, they moved six tables and twelve chairs, but they were large men, and they liked to sit in the corner. Was that so bad? Before the hostess could make her escape, the brothers put in a request.

"Could we have individual containers of sweet tea? And could you reserve a pie for each of us? Doesn't matter what flavor. Also, Corliss is going to need all of his food run through a blender 'cause he can't open his mouth. Thanks, sugar." Darcy raised his hand to pat her on the shoulder again, thought better of it, and dropped his hand.

The hostess nodded dazedly and hurried away.

"She's pretty," Darcy noted.

"Don't," Everett said. Hitting on waitresses was one definitive reason they had been tossed out of restaurants.

"I was just saying," Darcy said. They sat and waited impatiently for their waitress to arrive. Brent had his back to her, so he didn't understand why his brothers tensed and straightened as she approached. *She must be even prettier than the hostess,* he thought as he turned to her with a smile.

His smile faded only to be quickly replaced by anger. He jumped up, towering over her. "What are you doing here?"

"I'm working," she said, equally as furious.

"You're supposed to be in college," he fumed.

"I can't afford college."

"Your college is paid for," he told her.

"I'm not taking your money," she said, trying hard not to yell.

"Oh yes you are," he practically roared.

She glared up at him, standing on her toes to try and at least reach his shoulders. "I'm not taking your money, and you can't make me. I'll send another waitress to serve you." With that, she turned and stormed back into the kitchen.

Brent sat down, deflated.

"So that was Haley," Corliss muttered.

That was Haley, Brent thought. He sat, dazed, while conversation swirled around him. He knew her by sight, but they hadn't spoken since that horrible day fifteen years before. Not that he hadn't remained a part of her life, because he had. But he had taken a hands-off approach, figuring any direct contact would only traumatize her further.

He had planned her life accordingly, putting a little of his salary into savings for thirteen years until she turned eighteen, graduated, and went to college. Then he had his lawyer draw up the papers that transferred the account to her, to be used for the college of her choice. He hadn't checked to make sure his plan was being followed. Who in her right mind would give up a free ride to college? Haley, apparently.

His anger grew into full-blown rage as he waited, and then he could contain it no longer. He stood, pushing his chair back so the legs scraped loudly on the floor.

"I hope we get to eat before he gets us thrown out," Grant remarked as Brent stormed off in the direction of the kitchen.

The kitchen was tiny, and Haley wasn't in it, but he spotted a back exit. Not pausing or slowing his stride, he burst through the door and stepped into the cool night air.

Haley had her back against the building, her eyes squeezed tightly shut as if she were in pain. But when she opened them and glared at Brent, he saw no pain, only anger.

"What?" she snapped.

"You know what," he said. "Why aren't you in college?"

"I already told you. I'm not taking that money."

"That money is for your college."

She shook her head, a stubborn tilt to her chin.

"You are one hard-headed child," he said.

"I am not a child. I'm twenty."

He rolled his eyes. "I thought I knew everything when I was twenty."

"You still think you know everything," she returned.

He surprised her by laughing. "That's because now I actually do know everything, and I know that if you don't go to college, you're going to regret it someday."

"I will go to college," she said. "When I can pay for it myself."

"Working as a waitress? You'll be old and gray before you can afford it."

"I can go to a state school and get scholarships. I had good grades."

"You had excellent grades, which is why you shouldn't waste your potential."

Perhaps it shouldn't surprise her how closely he had kept tabs on her, but it still did. "You know about my grades?"

His index finger brushed her forehead, skimming aside a lock of honey-colored hair. "I know everything," he said.

She shuddered, sincerely hoping he was exaggerating. His hands settled on her shoulders and gave them a gentle squeeze. "What can I say to convince you to use the money, Haley? There must be something."

Haley bit her lip and searched his eyes. Her palms pressed lightly against his chest. "There's nothing, Brent. Nothing at all."

He frowned, puzzled by her unconvincing tone. There was something that would make her give in, but he didn't know what. Why wouldn't she tell him? Women were so confusing. Girls, he amended himself. Haley was forever a little girl in his mind.

"At least promise me you'll think about it," he said in the gentle tone he reserved for the horses. His thumbs smoothed over her shoulder bones.

She slowly shook her head. "I'll never change my mind about the money, Brent. Take it back and use it as a scholarship for someone who needs it."

"You need it," he said, his exasperation mounting again.

"Not from you."

He wanted to be angry with her, but for some reason his anger had burned itself out. In its place he felt…what? Confusion? But why should he feel confused? This was Haley, the little girl he had watched grow up for the last fifteen years. Maybe he was confused because they were talking like old friends when, really, they were strangers to each other. If not for that one horrific event that linked them indelibly together, they would be nothing to each other.

"You should go eat something, and I need to get back to work," she said softly.

He couldn't help but smile at her. "Stubborn girl," he said.

"Stubborn woman," she corrected, and then she sauntered away, leaving him staring after her.

When he returned to the table, he saw his brothers had already ordered for him, and the food had arrived. They had ordered one or two of everything on the menu so the table looked like a feast that had been prepared for King Henry VIII. And they were devouring the food with equal fervor.

Brent sat and joined in the fray, trying to allow the food to take his mind off Haley and her aggravating refusal to use her college money. His mind kept flashing back to her tone and the expression on her face as she said there was nothing he could say to make her take the money. Why had it seemed like she was waiting for him to say something that would change her mind? What could possibly work to force her to take the money?

He remained uncharacteristically quiet, not even joining in the debate his brothers waged over which was better, the chicken or the beef. The score was tied two to two and they were counting on Brent to be the tie breaker, but he had no opinion. For once his food tasted like sawdust and he had eaten on autopilot with no appreciation for his victuals. His brothers didn't comment. Even though they enjoyed teasing others, they never teased each other, especially about the things that were really bothering them. And they all knew the situation with Haley was really bothering Brent.

The waitress brought their check. They gave her a thirty percent tip. She had been friendly and smiling, even before they paid her, seeming to enjoy their antics and conversation.

"I think we're going to be able to come back here," Darcy said happily.

The brothers stood and rearranged the furniture they had confiscated, putting everything back in proper order. They quietly began filing out the door, Brent bringing up the rear, when he stopped, turned on his heel and stalked back inside.

Haley watched him approach, a dangerous gleam in his eye, and she steeled herself for another confrontation. He didn't argue with her, though, he simply picked her up, threw her over his shoulder, and carried her outside.

Darcy sighed and gave a sad shake of his head as he eyed the cafe. "I think it's safe to say we won't be welcome back there again after this."

CHAPTER 3

*H*aley didn't say a word as Brent carried her out of the restaurant, thrown over his shoulders like a sack of potatoes. The Honeywell brothers had a well-earned reputation for their crazy schemes. Once they had their minds made up, there was no changing them. Protesting would be futile. Besides, she was a little curious about what he intended to do with her.

Brent tossed the keys to his brother, Corliss. "You drive." He stepped up into the truck, grunting under the addition of Haley's weight. He set her down in his lap and buckled the seatbelt over both of them.

She was sideways facing Corliss. He smiled at her. "Don't worry, sugar. We always treat our captives well." He added a wink for good measure. She rolled her eyes.

Separately, the brothers could be quite charming. Together, they were redundant and overpowering. From a distance, they looked like quintuplets. Even up close it could be difficult to point out distinctive features among them. There were height differences, of course. At 6'5", Brent was the shortest. At 6'11", Everett was the tallest. The other brothers averaged somewhere between.

Haley wondered if the others smelled as good as Brent. Somehow, she thought not. His spicy scent had lingered on her hair for days after the accident, giving her something good to hold onto amongst all the horror.

She closed her eyes and inhaled, wanting to groan with the pain and futility of it all. He still smelled exactly the same, causing Haley to want to react as she had so long ago by flinging her arms around his neck and pressing her face to his chest.

In some ways, the situation was both her every dream come true and her worst nightmare. How long had she dreamed and hoped that Brent would swoop in and save her by taking her away from her horrible life? Well, that was an easy question to answer: for exactly fifteen years.

At first she had wanted him to adopt her and become her new caretaker, as her father had been. Then, when she grew older and realized he was little more than a kid himself, she had wanted him to be her big brother, to lay a protective arm around her shoulders and tell her everything was going to be okay.

Lately, the last few years, she plain wanted him. Not that she didn't date other men, because she did. In fact, she had been dating the same guy on and off since high school. But her heart belonged to Brent, and she feared it always would. Some days the pointlessness in the situation hit her anew and almost crushed her. Not only was he twelve years her senior, but he saw her as a child and always would. Her greatest fear was that someday he would marry and she would be forced to watch him with some other woman, lavishing someone else with the well of tenderness and affection she knew dwelled deep inside him.

The whole town thought the Honeywell men were a bunch of cavemen; the whole town was wrong. Haley knew because Brent had proved it to her, both on the day of the accident, and several times after. Every year without fail on her birthday, he sent her a bouquet of flowers. She would never forget the first time, her sixth birthday and the first without her father. It had been an awful day, and then the doorbell rang. The man on the other side bowed and handed her a beautiful bouquet with every color of zinnia, making her smile and laugh in delight.

For Christmas, he sent her gift cards, telling her to pick something for herself, every year but her sixteenth. That year, he had sent something special. And he didn't simply remember birthdays and Christmases. For homecoming and prom, he had sent bouquets of red roses along with notes reminding her that her date should treat her special because she was.

How could she not love him? For most of her life, he had been like a fairy godfather, providing her with much-needed care and encouragement from afar. Somehow in fifteen years, they had never spoken or met face to face. Until today. Now she sat on his lap with his hand pressed firmly to the small of her back for support. For her own sanity, she couldn't let him know how she truly felt. If he patronized her or, worse, pitied her for her feelings, she thought she might wither and die. Better to remain hostile and keep him at arm's length than let him know she had been in love with him for as long as she could remember.

Haley was tiny, and she was tense. She felt small and fragile, as if Brent could fit her in the palm of his hand. His thumb, gently smoothing up and down her spine, did nothing to soothe her. In fact, she seemed to be more tense as the miles stretched. He frowned, puzzled. His family was affectionate, but the simple touch seemed to bother Haley. His parents were huggers and kissers, and so were all their children. The brothers weren't affectionate with each other, of course, but they were with Ivy. Or they had been until she betrayed them all by moving to Montana. Their standard greeting for their baby sister had been to kiss her cheeks and toss her in the air. It still was whenever they saw her, only now her Yankee husband hovered disapprovingly in the background.

But Haley hadn't grown up like they had. As far as Brent could tell, her father had been the only loving influence in her life, and Brent had taken him away. Somehow he had to make that up to her or die trying. If he couldn't convince her to take the money and go to college, then he would have to think of something else.

❧

They arrived at the farm and Haley looked around in fascination. As a girl, she had dreamed of this place. It was beautiful and sprawling with horses everywhere. The brothers piled out of the truck, leaving Haley and Brent inside alone. Her neck muscles gave out before her pride, and she rested her head against his chest, staring at the idyllic farmhouse in front of them.

"What are you going to do with me now?" she asked.

"I hadn't thought that far in advance," he admitted. "I guess I want you to stay here a couple of days and think things over."

She sighed. She wouldn't change her mind, but it would do no good to once again inform Brent of that fact. "I don't have anything with me," she pointed out instead.

"Ivy left some things here, and we always keep extra toothbrushes for guests. Tomorrow, we'll go to town and pick up your overnight bag." He tightened his arms around her, giving her a light squeeze. "Cheer up; I think you'll have fun."

If his idea of fun was for her to eat her heart out with the dying dream that he might ever see her as more than a child, then, sure, the next two days would be fun.

"We can talk and catch up. Get to know each other again," he added.

Technically they had never known each other, but she knew what he meant. The events of that long ago day had bonded them, making them feel, at least temporarily, like a part of each other. Since that day, she had never thought of Brent as a stranger, even though they hadn't spoken a word in all that time.

"Why didn't you ever contact me? Why did you stay away?" she asked.

There it was; the question he had been dreading. "At first, I was in shock and trying to heal. Then I went away to college for four years."

Maybe that explained the first five years, but not the past ten. If he didn't want anything to do with her, he wouldn't have sent the gifts or cards. He would have stayed away completely. But had hadn't; he had made himself a part of her life, but not all the way. He had hovered on the periphery, there but invisible. She wanted to ask him more, but if she did, she might reveal her blatant yearning for him.

"Do you need to call your mom?" His palm began to smooth up and down her spine again. Was he trying to kill her?

"No," she said, her voice tight.

"I don't want her to worry."

"Why would she? I don't live with her."

His hand stilled. "You don't live with your mom?"

She shook her head. "I live in an apartment in Lexington."

"You live in Lexington?"

She tapped his chest. "Is this thing stuck on repeat?"

He clasped her hand and drew it away from his chest. "You are too young to live on your own in the city."

"Brent, I'm twenty. I've been living on my own for two years, and Lexington isn't exactly LA."

"Still," he said, frowning. After she turned eighteen and he handed over the account he had set up for her, he had sort of lost track, thinking she was safe and in college. Now he realized that for the last few years she had been on her own, working low-paying jobs and doing who knows what with her free time.

"Who are your friends? What do you do for fun?"

"I work. Otherwise, I go out with my boyfriend or occasionally hang out with my best friend from high school."

His frown increased. Her life sounded lonely and depressing. She was supposed to be having a great time at college, not living alone and figuring out how to pay the bills. How had he let this happen? How had he let her slip through the cracks of his careful planning?

Outside the temperature was dropping and the sun had set an hour ago, but inside the truck felt cozy and warm and Haley never wanted to leave. She couldn't quite resist the urge to snuggle closer to Brent, and so she did. He wrapped his arms more snuggly about her.

"Cold?" he asked.

"Hmm," she replied vaguely.

"We could go in," he suggested, but he also sounded like he was in no hurry to leave the truck. Not being an introspective person, he didn't puzzle over why sitting in the truck with Haley felt so nice; it just did, and he saw no reason to change the status quo.

"So you live in Lexington, you work at a diner, and you have a boyfriend," he recapped.

"That about sums it up. What about you? What's your life like?" She paused. "Do you have a girlfriend?"

He smiled at her tentative tone. If he didn't know better, he might think she had a little crush on him. "Not at present." In reality, it had been way too long since he dated someone. In college, he'd had no trouble getting girls. They had flocked to him, and he had dated several. Then he returned to his hometown, back to his brothers, and the well dried up. Puzzling.

"You're a young girl, Haley. You shouldn't be living like a sad old woman. You should be gaining the freshman fifteen, having wild times with your roommates, and learning a career."

"Brent, if you call me young one more time…"

"What? What can *you* do to *me*?"

She pulled back to look up at him and his smile froze. "I don't know what I can do, but I know what I can try."

Surely she didn't mean that the way it sounded. If he didn't know better, he might think she was trying to flirt with him. He laughed and reached up to ruffle her long hair. She caught his wrist and shook her head. "Don't," she commanded. They remained that way for a few beats with their arms gripped in midair, almost like a dance pose. The tension in the truck was suddenly palpable. Brent felt like a haze was lifting and he was beginning to see her for the first time. Long hair, big brown eyes, lips that…

"Your brothers said y'all kidnapped another girl, but I didn't believe them."

He turned to look at his mother now framed in the open doorway of the truck. "Mom, this is Haley Griffin. Haley, my mother, Mrs. Honeywell."

"How do you do, Mrs. Honeywell?" Haley asked politely. She dropped Brent's wrist, allowing her hand to fall listlessly to her lap.

"Probably much better than you right now, my dear," Mrs. Honeywell said. Her eyes shot back and forth between the pair in the truck, narrowing on her son who squirmed uncomfortably under her inspection. If there was one person on the planet who could make the Honeywell boys behave, it was their mother. "Y'all come inside and get comfortable." With a final suspicious glance around the interior of the truck, she shut the door and headed toward the house.

Brent hopped from the truck and turned his back to Haley. "Hop on, kiddo," he invited.

Haley took the proffered invitation with a roll of her eyes. *Kiddo?* If he offered to take her to the carnival and buy her some cotton candy, she wouldn't be held responsible for her actions.

<h1 style="text-align:center">CHAPTER 4</h1>

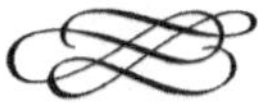

"So you snatched a waitress, right out of the restaurant?"

"Pretty much," Brent told his mother. She had sent Haley to her guestroom to get settled in, and now her sons were lined up on two couches in the living room while she interrogated them. She had repeated this scene with them so often over the years that she could say all the lines by heart, including theirs. They never seemed to understand the implications of their behavior.

She pinched the bridge of her nose and squeezed her eyes tightly shut. "You're all good boys, and I know it. Why can't you act like it?" Technically, they were men. They ranged in ages from twenty six to thirty two. But to her, and probably to the rest of the community, they would always be boys.

"But, Mom, she won't go to college," Brent said.

"Brent, you can't make someone do what she doesn't want to do. And you can't kidnap her as punishment." Long ago she had given up thinking that she shouldn't have to tell her sons things that should be obvious to others. For instance, that kidnapping was wrong. Did Frank and Jesse James' mother have days like this?

"It's not punishment," Brent argued. "I simply thought that if she had a couple of days to think things through, she might change her mind."

"In other words, you intend to browbeat her into submission," his mother said.

"She's a kid, Mom. She needs guidance."

Of all the clueless things he had said, that might top the list. Was he really trying to tell her that the lovely young woman down the hall, the one who hadn't stopped staring at him with star-struck doe eyes, was a child? "Brent," she said, shaking her head. "She's not a little girl anymore."

Brent looked up at her with soul-searing pain so deep in his eyes, she winced. "I want her life to go well, Mom. I want what's best for her."

"Oh, Brent," she said. All these years later, and he was still hurting over the accident that had taken Haley's father's life. How would he ever let go of the guilt? Guilt he should never have felt in the first place. Everyone agreed the accident hadn't been his fault. "I know you've tried to do right by her over the years, and it's made my motherly heart proud. But, honey, she's an adult now, and you have to let her go. Try to stop being her protector; try to be her friend instead."

Be friends with Haley? He didn't know why the thought should make him feel so odd, unless it was because she was so much younger. What could they possibly have in common except the worst day of their lives?

"I'm going to go check on her," he announced.

His mother let out a long sigh. She did that a lot, he realized. He wondered why. "Haley," he spoke as he tapped on her door. "It's me. Are you settling in okay? Do you need anything?"

She opened the door. A pair of Ivy's pajamas draped on her tiny frame. Ivy was tall for a girl, a good six inches taller than Haley. The pajamas dwarfed her. "Maybe those were maternity pajamas," he suggested when he saw her. Ivy had recently given birth to her first baby.

She crossed her arms self-consciously and prepared to close the door. He smiled and stepped forward. Taking her arm in his, he began to roll her sleeves. He had to roll them four times before he finally found her hands.

"Better," he said.

"Thank you," she said.

He leaned against the doorframe. "I'm surprised you're going to bed so early."

"I'm a morning person," she told him. She mimicked his pose, leaning against the doorframe so they were across from each other with the width of the doorframe between them. "Aren't you?"

"I'm an anytime person. I don't seem to require a lot of sleep."

"Somehow I could have guessed that," she said with a smile.

"Why's that?"

"More time to get into trouble."

He smiled. "What would you know about trouble, little bit?"

"Wouldn't you like to know," she said.

His smile fled at her cryptic tone. "Yes, I would. You don't party, do you? What do you and your friends do for fun? Is your boyfriend a good kid?"

She shook her head and laughed as she closed the door on his face and locked it for good measure. Brent stood on the other side, scowling at the door. Why hadn't he thought to take more of an interest in her life lately? Even if she was in college, she would need checked up on. He felt like somehow she had slipped under his radar and developed a life without his knowledge, and he didn't like that. When she was in high school, he had personally vetted all her dates, talking to the principal about what kind of kids they were. He had kept close tabs on her, reviewing her transcripts and searching for any clues that she might be in trouble.

But for some reason, he had allowed graduation to lull him into a false sense of security. Thinking his job was done, he let her go. Now he was regretting that mistake. What had Haley been doing the last two years, and who had she been doing it with? In the morning, he vowed he would get some answers.

True to her word, Haley woke early the next morning. Usually she rose before most people she knew, but not here. On a farm there must always be activity, because as soon as dawn broke the next morning the barns were already bustling with movement. She donned the clothes she had worn the night before, feeling gritty, and exited her room in search of coffee. Mrs. Honeywell had given her the tour of the grand house the night before, so she should have no trouble finding the kitchen, but there were eight bedrooms in the house, and Haley had to pause and get her bearings a couple of times before finding her way.

Everything in the house was huge, including the kitchen, and especially the wooden kitchen table that almost spanned the length of the room. Some of the family sat at the table, eating and talking. Brent was among them. He looked up with a welcoming smile and patted the seat beside him.

"Is it okay if I grab some coffee?" she asked.

"Sandy will get it for you," he replied. He signaled to a woman who was obviously their housekeeper. She poured a cup of coffee and set it in front of Haley.

Haley stared at it so her amazement wouldn't show. The only maid she had ever seen was Alice on *The Brady Bunch.* Everyone knew the Honeywells were rich, but Haley had never given the matter much thought before. Now that she was seeing their grandiosity up close and in person, she realized with dismay that it was one more league in the gulf between her and Brent. If he ever settled down, it would probably be with some other horse royalty because they all tended to marry each other.

"Something wrong, sugar?" Brent asked.

She looked up at him and shook her head. *No, I'm a rube who's hopelessly in love with someone completely out of her reach.* "Do you think we could go home today so I can get my things? I feel a little gross." She wrinkled her nose, wishing she hadn't pointed out her obvious deficiency.

"You look pretty as a picture to me," Brent said with a wink.

Thanks, Grandpa, she wanted to say. His paternal attitude was making her crazy. Haley dropped her eyes to her coffee again, glad for the reprieve. Sandy set a plate before her and the family passed steaming bowls to her so she could fill it. Unused to such a large breakfast, she took some fruit and eggs, bypassing the biscuits and bacon. When her light breakfast was finished, Brent rose and held out her chair to help her stand.

"Let's go, sugar." He walked behind her, whistling happily. They reached the truck and he lifted her into the passenger side, pausing with her in his arms when she was eye level. "You're as cute as pie, you know that, sugar?"

If he kissed the tip of her nose or pinched her cheek, she would punch him. But he didn't; he released her, tucking her safely into the truck. "Brent," she said as soon as they were on the road, "let's not do this."

"Do what?" he asked.

"I don't need to stay at the farm. I overheard your mom saying your sister was coming for a visit in a couple of days. I don't want to add stress or get in the way."

"You're not in the way, Haley," he said earnestly. "I want you there. Don't you want to be there? We've never really had a chance to spend time together, and now we have a chance."

Haley groaned and dropped her head in her hands. Brent pulled the truck to the side of the road. Unlatching his seatbelt, he slid across the seat and took her in his arms. "What is it, baby? Why don't you want to stay at the farm? Can't you tell me what's wrong?"

You're what's wrong, she wanted to say. *You call me 'baby' and 'sugar' and treat me like a beloved pet, but you don't want me in the same way I want you.* "Please don't make me stay."

"Of course I won't," he said soothingly. "You don't have to stay. We can go back to the way it was, when we never talked. We can be the kind of friends who never see each other. It's okay."

And now he was using guilt. He was a master manipulator. She groaned again and gave up the pretense of trying to hold herself away from him. Her forehead dropped to his chest with a thunk, and her arms slipped around his neck. "You're not playing fair."

She could feel his smile against the top of her head. He gave her waist a squeeze. "Come on, let's go get your stuff before you change your mind again." He slid behind the steering wheel and started the truck again. "And don't forget your swimsuit; we'll probably use the hot tub."

She spent the remainder of the ride trying to figure out if he was purposely messing with her head.

By the time they reached her apartment, Haley decided that, whether or not it was on purpose, Brent was messing with her head. And it was time for a little payback.

Yesterday when he carried her out of the diner, she had been working a double shift. Any makeup she'd applied was long gone. Her hair was in a disheveled ponytail, and she had been wearing her uniform—pleated khaki pants with an ill-fitting knit shirt. To say she hadn't looked good would be putting it mildly. All that was about to change.

"Do you mind if I shower while we're here?" she asked.

"Go ahead," he urged. "That will give me time to rifle through your things and see what you've been up to."

She would have laughed if she thought he was kidding. Since she knew he wasn't, she waved her hand wearily toward her living room. Short of taking all her possessions into the bathroom with her, there was no way to stop him from snooping. Maybe the bathroom wouldn't be enough to stop him; Brent wasn't big on knowing his boundaries.

The hot spray of the shower felt wonderful as it worked to wash off dirt, grit, and food smell, along with some of her anxiety and confusion. There was a good chance Brent would never see her as anything but a child, but that didn't mean she had to act like one. She was an independent woman who was used to taking care of herself. Now was the time to start acting like it.

Her pep talk continued while she was drying her hair and applying makeup. She had never been one of those girls who wore tight clothing to attract male attention, so she chose a pair of comfortable jeans and a sweater. But by the time she emerged from the bathroom, she felt good, and she knew she looked good.

"I packed before I showered, so I'm ready when you are," she announced.

Brent was rifling through her desk. He turned to her with a smile that froze. "What?" he murmured.

"I said I'm ready. Are you ready, Brent?" She fisted her hands on her hips, making the words a challenge. If he was going to bully her into staying with him, then she was going to do her best to change things between them.

"R-ready?" he said.

She smiled, certain that Brent Honeywell had never stammered in his life. "I do have one question, though. Be right back." She darted to her room and returned with two items in her hands. "You said to bring a suit, but I need your opinion. This bikini is what I usually wear for sunbathing, but I know your family is conservative, so I didn't want to offend." She held up the pretty bikini in front of her. It wasn't scandalously tiny, but it was still a bikini. "Or there's this one piece." She moved the bikini and replaced it with the one piece.

He blinked, dazed, before quickly turning from her to stare at the wall. "The one piece," he said.

"The one piece it is," she said cheerfully. "Thank you." The poor dope hadn't realized it was a trick question all along. She had been pretty sure he wouldn't want her parading in a bikini in front of his brothers. But what he didn't realize was that she looked even better in the forgiving, flattering white one piece. Her frumpy one piece, the green one, was tucked safely in the back of her drawer; that one had never been an option.

She was in her bedroom retrieving her overnight bag when Brent stepped in. "You should pack for longer. Stay a week," he said.

She dropped the bag and spun to look at him. "A week?" she croaked. Keeping up the pretense of being in charge of her emotions was something she could handle for a day, at best. Being subjugated to him for an entire week was too much to contemplate.

"A week," he repeated. "What's the big deal?"

"I have a job," she sputtered.

"No you don't. I checked your voicemail. You got fired for, and I quote, 'associating with those hooligan Honeywells.'" He sprawled on her bed and smiled up at her.

"You got me fired?" she said accusingly. "I needed that job."

"Why do you need a job? You have a lot of money in your bank account."

She pressed her thumb to the center of her forehead, trying to ward off a budding headache. "No, you have a lot of money in my bank account. I haven't touched it, and I won't. And now I need to spend this week hunting for another job."

"Why are you a waitress anyway? Is that what you enjoy doing?"

"Of course not," she said. She hated waitressing, the aching feet, rude customers, and cloying food smell were enough to make anyone cranky at the end of the day. But she was a high school graduate. What hope did she have of getting a good job?

"Tell you what," he said. "Stay the week with us. If you still decide not to go to college, then I will help you find a better job. It may surprise you to learn that the Honeywell name carries some weight in the community." He grinned up at her from his vantage point on her bed. Even though the bed was a double and she sometimes felt lost in it, Brent dwarfed it with his massive body. His bed had to be a king, or else his feet would dangle over the end.

"Your sister is coming," she pointed out. "I don't want to be in the way."

"You're not in the way; I keep telling you. We have guests all the time. That's why we have a guestroom. You can meet my baby niece." He said the words tauntingly, as an inducement, and they worked.

"A baby?" she echoed.

He nodded. "She's the prettiest baby I've ever seen," he said earnestly. "Thankfully she looks everything like Ivy and nothing like the Yankee she married."

"You don't like your sister's husband?"

"He's a Yankee," he said, as if that explained everything.

"But is he a good man? Does he love your sister and make her happy? Does he provide for her?"

"He's a Yankee," Brent stubbornly repeated.

"Oh, Brent," she said. "You're hopeless." She reached down to squeeze his ankle. He smiled, extended his hand, and pulled her onto the bed beside him. Then, realizing what he had done and where they were, jumped up as if she were a live wire. In one motion, he caught her overnight bag and bounded out of the room.

"I'll wait out here while you finish packing," he called.

She smiled at the door, thinking things were going even better than she could have hoped. Had anyone ever made Brent nervous before? She didn't think so. Being nervous was a good sign, in her opinion. It meant he was becoming confused, and confusion was better than his patronizing condescension that made her want to scream. She finished packing in short order after belatedly including a couple of dresses. With the Honeywells, one never knew what to expect. The dresses might come in handy, if only for church.

Brent was once again looking relaxed as he sat on her sofa and leafed through a scrapbook she had made. "Why did you move away from your mother?" he asked. His tone conveyed concern, and Haley almost smiled.

He had grown up safe, protected, and loved by two parents and a gaggle of siblings. He was also thirty two and still lived at home. He had no idea what it meant to be alone. "My mom wasn't abusive," she prefaced. "But sometimes scorching indifference is as bad. After my dad died, it was like I ceased to exist. She fed and clothed me, but that was it. There was no warmth, affection, or attention. She was into her life, her friends, and her job. She routinely went out every weekend, and I learned to be alone."

"She left you alone when you were six?" he asked, outraged.

Haley nodded, a sad smile on her face. "Fortunately for her, I was a good, capable kid who didn't get into trouble."

"If I had known…" Brent said, trailing off.

"If you had known, then what, Brent?" Haley asked. "You were a kid in college. What could you have done?"

"Something," he said helplessly. He seemed so upset, as if her life was somehow his responsibility.

She reached out and pressed her palm to his cheek, his ever-present beard stubble cutting into her hand. "My life is not your fault. Stop trying to pretend it is."

He closed his eyes and leaned in to her touch. "But your dad, he loved you."

"My dad loved me. I was his world. And that love is what carried me through the remainder of my childhood." She bit her lip, trying to work up the courage to say what she needed to say next. "My dad and you, that is. You were a reminder of him, a reminder that someone, some-where was looking out for me. You made a dreary life cheerful, and for that I thank you." She finished speaking in a tremulous whisper.

He opened his eyes and pressed his hand over hers, swallowing it whole with his massive paw. The look in his eyes was intense. Tension bounced and hummed between them, but neither of them made a move to do anything about it. "Don't thank me," he said at last. His voice sounded choked. He turned his head and pressed his lips to her palm. "Take the money," he said, his mouth moving against her hand.

She shook her head.

There was a moment when she wasn't sure what was going to happen next. Brent seemed to be wavering between anger and temp-tation. At last he smiled, stood, and picked her up under one arm like a football. "You're a stubborn kid, you know that?" He grabbed her suitcase and bounded out of the apartment, oblivious to her calls to be put down.

When they were finally packed and in his truck, it was almost noon.

"Want to grab some lunch, sugar?" he asked.

Haley cringed at the endearment. The Honeywells called all women "sugar" or "darlin'" or something equally as outdated and misogynistic. For Brent to use it on her meant she wasn't anything special, she was some girl. "Sure," she said lamely.

He mistook her lack of enthusiasm as lack of hunger. "You're going to have to develop an appetite if you stay with us." For good measure, he reached over and gave her waist a pinch. "You're tinier than a newborn colt."

"That's strange. My boyfriend tells me I have an awesome figure. You must have differing tastes in women."

He dropped his hand and gripped the steering wheel with a frown. "I don't like that kind of talk from your boyfriend."

Haley laughed. "I'll tell him you said so."

"I'm serious," he said. "You're not an object to be ogled, Haley."

"Let me see if I have this right: It's okay for you to tell me I look like a newborn colt and pinch my waist, but it's not okay for my boyfriend to tell me he likes my body."

"That's different," he said.

"How is it different?"

"He's a stupid kid, and I'm your…" He trailed off, his frown intensifying.

"Yes? You're my what? What exactly are you to me, Brent?"

"I'm your…guardian angel," he finished, immensely pleased with the description.

Haley laughed again. "You are nobody's idea of an angel." With his dark hair and eyes, massive size, and prankster attitude, he was more devilish than angelic.

"I am a perfect angel," he said with mock innocence.

"Yes, I'm sure it's your angelic demeanor that's gotten you thrown out of so many restaurants. My manager practically had apoplexy when she ran back to the kitchen to tell us the Honeywells had arrived."

"You're exaggerating," he said. "People love us."

She let the comment slide because he truly believed it and, therefore, there would be no changing his mind.

"So you knew it was us you were coming to wait on, and yet you still came," he said.

She shifted uncomfortably. "I drew the short straw."

He grinned. "Admit it, you wanted to see me."

"Now why would I want to see the mysterious stranger who dropped into my life, stayed there for fifteen years, and never showed me his face after that first day? A girl would have to be crazy to want to satisfy her curiosity about someone who sent her a lawyer's letter saying he was giving her a bank account with two hundred thousand dollars in it. Yes, I guess I'm that crazy curious." She crossed her arms over her chest and stared out the window.

"You're mad about the money," he drawled, darting her a disbelieving glance.

"Of course I'm not mad about the money, Brent. It's the nicest thing anyone has ever done for me. Everything you've ever done for me is the nicest thing anyone has ever done for me," she said. Tears sprang to her eyes and she stared toward the window again, willing them away.

"You sure sound mad," he said.

She sighed. How could she possibly explain to him her odd mix of emotions? She was touched and humbled by his gifts, but now that she was a woman, she didn't want the gifts; she wanted him. The money was beyond generous, but it was also a way of buying her off, of bowing out of her life. She couldn't make him stay, but she didn't want him to go. All in all, the situation was rife with emotional turmoil and confusion. For him, giving her the money meant severing all emotional ties. But for her, taking the money meant entangling herself even more because how could she accept such a massive gift and have it mean nothing? She was already in love with him; she didn't want to feel beholden to him, too.

She reached across the seat and laid her hand gently on his leg. "I'm not mad, Brent, honest I'm not," she said softly. "I will forever be grateful for everything you've done for me."

They apparently reached their lunch destination because he pulled into a parking space and turned off the truck. "Don't," he choked. "Don't be grateful to me, Haley. I'm only doing what I should. I wish I could do so much more."

"Why?" she asked, hating to see him in such obvious pain.

He shook his head, trying to clear it, and forced a smile. "Because you're worth it, sugar. Now let's get some food in you."

CHAPTER 6

Haley decided to let him get away with his evasive answer because, really, what choice did she have? None, and that was always the way with Brent. He was always the one with the control, always the one calling the shots. He was older, richer, and more powerful, both physically and in personality. And the thing was, most of the time she really didn't mind. She had been on her own so long that it was nice to have someone else call the shots for a while.

However, her woman's heart told her there was a difference in allowing a man to take charge and allowing a man to treat her like a child. One gave her a safe and protected feeling; the other made her want to throw a tantrum like the child he thought she was. How was she to make him understand the difference?

"Coming?" Brent asked. He opened her door and stood waiting.

"Sure," she said, forcing a smile of her own.

The restaurant was a bistro, full of leather and wood, where the specialty was steak and the portions were large. Brent excused himself to wash up, and Haley pulled out her phone to check her voicemail.

A message from her on again, off again boyfriend began to play, and she simultaneously smiled while feeling guilty. They weren't serious, but they were good friends, and she knew he wanted more from their relationship. She liked him as well as she could anyone, but her heart would never be free to give to anyone as long as there was Brent. The next message did not make her smile.

"What's the frown for, sugar?" Brent asked when he came back to the table.

"A message from my mother's boyfriend."

He frowned. "Why would your mother's boyfriend call you?"

"He wants your money," she said.

"My money? What are you talking about?"

"He somehow found out about the money in your account, and he wants it, I think."

"He wants your money?"

"No, he wants your money," she repeated patiently as she scanned the menu.

He snatched the menu out of her fingers. "Haley, tell me what he said to you. Has he threatened you?"

"No, of course not. He's a financial planner and he wants me to turn control of the money over to him so he can, in his words 'make it grow.' But I don't trust him, so I keep ignoring his insinuations."

His frown didn't waver. "Maybe I need to have a little talk with him."

She rested her hand on his forearm. "Brent, don't. It's nothing I can't handle. He's been perfectly polite; I don't much care for him. Let it go--don't search for trouble where there isn't any."

"I'm not searching for trouble," Brent said. "I don't like the thought of this man hounding you."

"He's not hounding." She set aside the menu and folded her arms on the table, leaning forward. "You know what your problem is?"

He mimicked her pose, leaning forward until their faces were only a few centimeters apart. "Why do I have the feeling you're going to tell me?"

"You're possessive," she said.

"Protective," he amended. "You need a protector—that's me."

"No, it's not only me. It's your sister, too. The way you talk about her husband like he's a bank robber and she's his hostage. They're married. They have a child together, you know."

"He's a Yankee," he said.

"Brent, we live in northern Kentucky. Did it ever occur to you that people in the Gulf States consider us Yankees?"

"We have accents," he said sullenly.

"My point is that you think you know what's best for everyone, and your stubborn refusal to admit otherwise is maddening."

"I do know what's best for everyone," he countered. "At least the people I care about, like you and Ivy."

"I appreciate that," she said, running her fingers gently over his arm. "But what you fail to realize is that, unlike Ivy, I am not your sister."

"You're my..." he trailed off, floundering.

"What? What am I? What is the end of the sentence?" she asked. Was his inability to pin a label on her somehow significant?

He captured her hand and twined their fingers together. "You're my girl," he said with a sweet smile.

Haley wanted the words to mean something, but she wasn't sure they did. He was generous with his affection and endearments. Were they mere words to him? Was the touch of his hand a casual gesture? They were so close as they leaned toward each other over the table that she could see the fine lines that were beginning to settle around his eyes when he smiled. Since she was trying to play down the age difference between them, she didn't think she should draw attention to them, but she couldn't stop herself from gently tracing them with her finger.

His eyelids fluttered with the proximity of her finger, but when that finger trailed to his mouth and began to trace the outline, he sucked in a breath and froze before clearing his throat.

"Haley," he began. He was going to tell her to stop, she knew it, but he didn't get the chance because the waitress arrived to take their order. They broke apart to place their order, and when the waitress left, Brent changed the subject.

"What are you going to study when you go to college?" he asked.

"I'm hoping to get my MRS," she declared. She wasn't really, but his avoidance of anything relating to them irritated her.

"Haley, you can't go to school to get a husband," he began. And then he lectured her until their food arrived. Haley tuned him out by staring at his lips as he talked. His lips were beautiful, full and kissable. Somehow she knew without trying that the prickly stubble around his mouth would chafe her skin. Absently, she rubbed at her chin, imagining the rash.

"Something wrong?" he asked at last.

"What?" she repeated, startled out of her daydream.

"You're rubbing your chin. Does it itch?"

"Not yet," she said.

Fortunately their food arrived before he could try and decipher her meaning.

"I think you must be a lucky charm," Brent said as they were leaving the restaurant. "The waitress actually smiled at me, and no one told me not to come back again."

"Does that ever happen to you when you're not with your brothers?" she asked.

"No, I guess now that you mention it that only happens when we're together. But why would it? We leave good tips."

How could she tell him that restaurant stories were notorious where the Honeywells were concerned? He honestly had no idea that going into the kitchen to check on the chef's progress, or ordering a restaurant's entire supply of a special, or any of the other things they did when they were together was unusual.

"Did you guys really tear out a wall in the Pioneer Café?" she asked.

"Now, see, when you say it like that, it sounds bad. Someone mentioned they were thinking of doing it anyway, and we were trying to determine if it was a load-bearing wall for them. How were we to know the person who made the comment was a customer and not the owner? And we did pay to have it fixed."

"And you have no idea why waitresses faint at the sight of you," she prompted.

He shook his head, still looking puzzled.

She laughed and squeezed his bicep. "Oh, Brent. You're hopeless."

"You didn't," he said.

"I didn't what?' she asked, confused.

"You didn't faint at the sight of us. You said your manager came to the kitchen and said we had arrived, and yet you still came to wait on us."

"You were sitting at my table," she hedged.

He shook his head. "Admit it, Haley. You wanted to see me that night." They reached the truck and stood facing each other next to the passenger door.

Of course she had wanted to see him; she was dying of curiosity about him, but his tone alleged something more, as if he were trying to prompt her to admit her feelings ran deeper than curiosity. No way was she going to go there. "You were assigned to my table," she reiterated.

She jumped, startled, when he reached out and brushed her neck with his fingers. "And this? Do you wear this because we were assigned to your table?" He held the locket between his fingers, making it sparkle as the sun bounced off it.

"Why did you buy it for me if you didn't want me to wear it?" she snapped, embarrassed at having been found out. She snatched it from his fingers and tucked it under her sweater.

"I didn't say I didn't want you to wear it; I'm glad you like it. Do you wear it every day?" There it was again—that calculating light in his eyes that made her think his question meant more than the words would have her believe.

She had worn the locket every day since the Christmas he gave it to her, the Christmas when she turned sixteen. She would never forget her excitement over the present—the shock when she realized he had sent her something different than his usual gift card, the joy when she realized it was jewelry. No one else had ever given her jewelry.

He smiled. Apparently her lack of answer meant as much as any answer she might have given. He reached out again and this time gently touched her earlobe.

"Wh-what are you doing?" she asked, disconcerted by the soft caress.

"Checking to see if your ears are pierced. I'm thinking it's time for matching earrings." With that, he lifted her into the truck, and they drove away.

"What do you want to do today?" he asked a few miles out of Lexington. Haley was having a difficult time shifting her mood from the strangely intimate locket conversation. But apparently Brent wasn't. His tone was casual, and so was the question.

"You tell me," she said. "Don't you have to work?"

He shrugged. "I have a loose schedule. They'll call if they need me."

"What exactly do you do?" she asked.

"I help with the horses; we all do. But then we each have other jobs that help with the business structure of the farm. I do all the legal work."

She stared, dumbfounded. "You're a lawyer?"

"Not technically—I didn't take the bar. I can't practice for other people, but I did go to law school, and so I do all my family's legal footwork." He smiled. "My dad is a shrewd businessman. He figured it was cheaper to send one of his sons to law school than it was to keep paying lawyer fees. And, fortunately, I had an interest in law."

He sounded so matter of fact about it, but she would bet that very few people knew he was a lawyer. Everyone knew he went to Georgetown for his undergrad, but most people assumed his father's money had gotten him in. But to become a lawyer, he must have been a smart and dedicated student, something that didn't fit her image of him. Maybe he preferred it that way. He certainly did nothing around town to make people think he was a studious bookworm.

"I surprised you," he guessed.

"You don't act very lawyerly," she said.

He quirked an eyebrow at her. "Lawyers can't have a good time?"

"Lawyers shouldn't get community service for defacing public property," she returned.

He waved his hand dismissively. "That statue looks better white, and everyone knows it. Judge Harper has a grudge against us because we toilet papered his chamber after the first time we were arrested."

She shook her head at him.

"What?" he asked.

"I was thinking about your son," she said.

"Do I have one I don't know about?" he asked.

"No, I mean your future son. You do realize that you're going to get all your bad behavior rebounded on you, right?"

"Bad is in the eye of the beholder," he said. "I see a need, I fill it."

"Nevertheless, you're going to have your hands full when you have children." The words made her sad as she pictured little dark-haired babies, the product of some other woman. She turned to stare at the passing landscape, her smile gone.

Sensing her sadness, he reached over to clasp her hand. "Who says I'll have kids? I might die a lonely old bachelor."

"Then that would be a waste of a very good man," she said gravely.

"I thought you said I was bad," he reminded her.

"Bad is in the eye of the beholder," she said, giving his hand a squeeze.

CHAPTER 7

"Let's ride," Brent suggested as soon as they deposited Haley's things in her room.

Immediate panic slammed her gut, causing it to clench and twist. "Now would be a good time to tell you that I'm terrified of horses," she said. She hated to make the admission, since horses were his livelihood, but she needed to be honest.

"Nonsense," he said. "Have you ever actually been near a horse?"

"Well, no, but they're huge and scary."

"See? You only think you're afraid. Come on." He grasped her hand and led her behind him at a trot, not giving her the chance to back out. He took her to one of the family's huge, beautiful barns. Everything on their farm was so white and pristine, from the mansion-like house to the bevy of barns to the acres and acres of fencerow.

Haley stood back, wide eyed, as Brent led a giant horse from one of his stalls. Or her stalls, Haley didn't know how to tell the difference. "Let's go," Brent said.

"Where's the saddle?" Haley asked. She wasn't an expert, but even she knew they needed a saddle.

"I prefer to ride bareback," Brent said.

"Somehow I could have guessed that," she murmured. Out loud she said, "Look, Brent, I'm happy you have confidence in my abilities, but I don't think I'm up to this."

"Nonsense, sugar," he said. And before she could protest further, he picked her up and tossed her onto the horse. She spent a terrified second alone on the horse, and then Brent was sitting behind her.

"You didn't think I meant for you to ride alone, did you?" he asked.

She had thought that, but she didn't admit it now. She was too relieved by his reassuring presence to answer. His arms fastened around her as he grabbed the bridle and he began talking softly in her ear.

"The key to riding a horse bareback is balance. In some ways, it's like riding a bike. You have to find your center of gravity and use it to direct the horse. Put your feet there." He pointed to a groove behind the horse's front legs. "Don't let your calves touch her sides; that's cheating. Don't look at the horse, look at the horizon. There, that's it," he said encouragingly, although she was sure he was the one actually in control of the horse, his praise made her feel more confident.

"Now, when you want to turn, look in that direction first. The horse will feel the shift and understand that's the way he's supposed to go."

She couldn't imagine ever needing to know this information, but she listened attentively anyway. Then he handed her the reins.

"Try it out," he commanded.

She stared at the leather in her hands, her panic returning once again.

"Easy, sugar," Brent soothed. Haley wasn't sure if he was talking to her or the horse until he rested his palm on her thigh and gave it a squeeze. "You've got this."

With his encouragement ringing in her ears, she gripped the reins tighter and tried to remember all that he'd told her. "Keep going straight, horse," she commanded. "Good girl," she said when they didn't veer off their course. Behind her, Brent chuckled softly and rested his other hand on her other thigh.

"It's kind of nice to have someone else in the driver's seat. Frees my hands up for other things," he said. His voice rumbled soft and low in her ear, turning her insides to molten lava. She began to wonder if maybe he really was trying to kill her. How else to explain why he put her on a horse, told her to concentrate, and then did everything in his power to make sure she couldn't concentrate?

"Haley," he whispered, his hands still solidly on her legs, and his mouth very close to her ear.

"Hmm," she whispered. She leaned into him, enjoying his warmth on her back.

"I think you've got this," he whispered, and then he was gone. His hands left her as they slipped to the horse's back. He vaulted off the horse, leaving her alone on top. She stared at him, openmouthed, as he grinned up at her from the ground.

"You're doing great," he said.

Surprise caused her to jerk the reins to the left, and then she was lying on the ground, looking up. They were in the middle of a lush pasture with grass so thick it felt like carpet, so she wasn't hurt. But she was dazed. Brent lay beside her and pressed his hand to her forehead.

"I don't get it; that trick worked when I taught Ivy to ride," he said, frowning.

She blinked up at him, too bewildered by the fall to decide if he truly was trying to kill her. "How old was she?" she asked dazedly.

"Three," he said.

She imagined poor little Ivy as a three year old, terrified and alone as her giant older brother stuck her on a horse barebacked and then jumped off. But try as she might, she couldn't muster pity for Ivy, only amusement. How she had survived her brothers was both a mystery and a miracle. She started to laugh, wiping away tears of amusement and pain.

Brent smiled and smoothed his hand over her forehead. "Are you okay?"

"I think so," she said.

He continued smoothing his hand over her head. "I like your hair," he commented. "You've kept it long all these years; you look like you did the day I found you."

They both frowned, he because he had rehashed a painful memory, and she because he was once again referring to her as a child.

His fingers trailed to the ends of her hair and brushed her neck. Haley snapped her head to the side, blocking access to her neck and trapping his fingers against her shoulder. She realized her mistake as soon as it happened.

"You're ticklish?" he guessed, a devilish grin on his face.

"No," she lied.

"You are," he said. "I can tell, and you know what's going to happen now, don't you?"

"Don't do it," she said. She tried to make the words sound like a command, but they ended up sounding like a plea.

He didn't respond. Instead, he captured her hands, pinning them to the ground. Then he leaned over her, forced her head to the side, and bit her neck exactly where she was most ticklish, as if he had a sixth sense about where to inflict the most torture. Haley laughed convulsively and would have flailed wildly if he hadn't secured her to the ground. Being Brent, he didn't stop at once. He bit her repeatedly until she was shrieking, gasping, and begging for mercy.

"Can't breathe," she gasped. "Please..." She would have said more, but she couldn't get enough air. He tickled her until she was in agony, and then he released her, rolling away to watch her laughter die down with a smile.

"You're so mean," she gasped as she wiped her eyes with the edge of her sleeve.

"What's mean about making someone laugh?" he asked.

"You wouldn't understand if you're not ticklish," she said. "It's more pain than pleasure."

His smile didn't waver because in his mind laughter equaled enjoyment. He had made her laugh, and that made him happy. "You're pretty," he blurted. "Really, really pretty." He reached out to touch her hair again, enjoying the softness. She smelled like strawberries.

Haley shook her head, sure he was still teasing her. Her face must be beet red from the exertion of laughing so hard. Her nose and eyes were running, and she could only guess that her hair now looked like a tangled bird's nest. "You're trying to be nice to me so I'll forgive you," she said.

"Forgive me for what?' he asked.

Should she try to explain to him, again, that being tickled wasn't pleasant for her? No, he would never understand. "Forget it," she said. She rolled to her side so they were facing each other. She pillowed her hands under her head and returned his smile. "It's very peaceful here," she commented. "This must have been a wonderful place to grow up."

"It was," he said. "I should have had you here much sooner than this." His smile dimmed.

She touched his cheek. "Brent, don't, please," she said.

"But you could have ridden the horses. Kids love horses," he said.

"I think if you had tried to teach me to ride any sooner, there's a good chance I wouldn't have lived through the experience," she said. "My bones needed this time to develop properly."

He laughed. "What a thing to say, Haley," he said. "I would never let anything bad happen to you."

She pointed to the horse a few yards away, now furiously nipping the lush grass as if trying to enjoy her freedom before the humans realized she was having fun. "I fell off that thing."

"So? Falling off horses is a part of life."

Now it was her turn to laugh. "Brent," she said, smoothing her hand over his cheek. "You're never dull, you know that?"

He turned his head slightly and pressed his lips to her palm, kissing it. "You're pretty good at rolling with the punches," he said. Most women he had dated either spent their time arguing with him or lecturing him. He never seemed to be able to please any of them, and he could never understand why. Why did women get upset over such little things? But Haley had been kidnapped and thrown off a horse and only expressed mild exasperation. Of course, she was a kid. Maybe that was the difference. Maybe when she grew up, she would dislike him. He hoped not.

"You're frowning," she noted.

"I was thinking I don't want you to change," he blurted. He never could seem to filter his thoughts before they leapt out of his mouth, another thing most women disliked. But Haley smiled.

"I'll try to give you fair warning before making any major changes to my person," she said.

They lay there, looking and smiling at each other for a few more minutes. An odd sort of tension crept between them. Brent couldn't seem to put a name to the feeling that kept popping up when he was with Haley, but he didn't like it. It made him feel uncomfortable for reasons he couldn't comprehend. This was Haley; why should things feel weird with her?

Her finger trailed to his lower lip as she gently traced the outline of his mouth, and he jumped away from her as if he had been branded. In one fluid motion, he was on his feet and calling to his horse. He heard Haley sigh, but decided to ignore it.

"Please tell me I'm not getting back on that thing," she said.

"The old adage is true, sugar. Getting back on again is the only way not to be afraid."

"Well then what are we waiting for, *sugar?*" she asked with forced enthusiasm. He laughed and lifted her onto the horse before vaulting on behind her. As soon as he was settled, she clutched at his arm. "Don't leave me alone this time," she said, all traces of amusement gone from her tone.

"I won't leave you alone," he promised. Cinching his arm around her waist, he signaled to the horse, and they were off.

CHAPTER 8

"It's supposed to be downright chilly tonight," Everett commented as the family ate supper in their massive kitchen.

"So it is," Darcy agreed.

Brent surveyed his brothers with a suspicious glower. They were up to something, and if he had to guess, he would say it involved Haley. If he didn't know better, he might think they found her attractive. But that was impossible. Not because she wasn't pretty, because she was. But she was a child; surely they could see that, couldn't they?

"Nice night for a soak in the hot tub," Everett said.

"So it is," Darcy agreed. Both turned to look at Haley.

"You brought your suit didn't you, Haley?" This came from Corliss.

"I did; Brent made sure of it." She turned a beaming smile on Brent, which he didn't return. Clearly, he hadn't thought through the ramifications of Haley in a bathing suit. His brothers liked women--that was no secret--but he had assumed they would realize Haley was off limits because of her age. When she excused herself to go change, he turned scathing eyes on them.

"She's twenty," he hissed.

"That's legal plus two," Corliss said.

"No way," Brent said.

"Have you looked at her?" Darcy asked. "I mean really looked?"

"She's a girl," Brent said.

"The girl is a woman, and she is mighty fine," Grant said. His gaze strayed toward Haley's bedroom.

Brent frowned. Of all his brothers, Grant was the closest to her in age, but at twenty six, that was still six years too old. He left to go change into his trunks, hurrying in order to beat his brothers to the hot tub. But he didn't; by the time he arrived, they were all there and staring toward the door as if waiting for a Broadway play.

The suspense didn't lessen when Haley entered wearing one of the plush white bathrobes the family provided for guests. Her hair was fastened in a loose braid that hung down the middle of her back. One dainty foot slipped out and then another as she removed her sandals. Her back was to the tub as she took off the robe and draped it over a chair. Then she turned and blinked self-consciously when she realized the brothers were collectively staring at her. They turned away, conversing among themselves and giving her a reprieve, all except Brent. He remained staring, speechless.

The suit was modest. Everything was covered, as much as it could be by a bathing suit. Why, then, did she look so *good*? She was perfect —perfect body and perfect complexion. Somehow even though it was autumn, she still appeared sun kissed. He realized she was still hovering uncertainly at the edge of the tub, and he snapped to attention.

"Come in, it's cold out," he said. He reached out a hand to help her in and kept it, drawing her protectively closer to him once she was safely inside the tub. Looking like this, he didn't trust her near any other male, and especially not his brothers. But what could he say? He had chosen this suit. When he thought of how much worse things might be if she had worn the bikini, he almost wanted to groan. Why did she have to be so alluring? He felt irrationally irritated with her for her beauty. If she were ugly, it would be easier to remember that she was out of his reach.

"You're quiet," Haley said. She was learning that a quiet Brent was much more dangerous than a loud one.

"Am I?" he asked. He didn't look at her. Instead, he kept his gaze on his brothers, scanning the circle with a scowl.

"I've never been in a hot tub when it's cold outside," she remarked. The whirlpool was located adjacent to the large deck on the back of the house. But it wasn't a hot tub like any she had ever seen; it was at least fifteen feet long and ten feet across, more like a swimming pool, really. She supposed with five men who all averaged near seven feet tall, a larger tub was in order.

The crisp air caused steam to rise from the surface of the bubbling tub. Haley felt the hair around her face begin to curl with the humidity. As a rule, her hair was more wavy than curly, but the tiny wisps near her face tended to spiral when damp. Brent's silence was making her nervous, but she didn't want to harp on it. She scanned the group of brothers, hoping to start a conversation, but each of them was looking studiously in another direction. Was she making them uncomfortable? Since their sister left, there probably hadn't been much of a female presence on the farm. Maybe they wished her gone.

"Maybe this was a bad idea," she muttered. She stood, but Brent grasped her wrist to hold her back.

"Wait," he said. "Don't go."

"Are you sure? It doesn't seem like you want me."

"I do want you to stay," he said. He tugged until she sat again. "Tell me something."

"What?"

"Anything. Tell me anything about your life. What was the last movie you saw in the theater?"

"It's been so long, I don't remember."

He frowned. "Why has it been so long?"

She shrugged. Movies were expensive, and she didn't like going on her own. "The downfall of being an old-fashioned girl is that I wait for someone to ask me to go. No one has asked in a long time."

"I thought you have a boyfriend," he said.

"Sort of," she replied.

"How can you sort of have a boyfriend?"

"We go out when neither of us has anything better to do."

"And he doesn't ever take you to the movies?" he asked.

She thought hard, trying to remember if Tyler had ever taken her to a movie. "Maybe when we first started dating in high school."

Brent shook his head. "That's not right, Haley. You should be with someone who treats you better, someone who cherishes you."

"What about you, Brent?"

He looked up sharply. "What do you mean?"

"You're good at doling out relationship advice, but you don't seem to be in one."

"Oh." He relaxed perceptibly and shrugged. "I date occasionally."

"Haven't you ever been serious with anyone?"

He shook his head again. "Nothing ever seems to stick, you know? I keep thinking when it happens, I'll know. Like a lightening bolt to the heart or something."

So he was a lawyer and a romantic. "The things I'm learning about you today," she said.

He smiled. "See? That's what you need; you need a man who surprises you."

"And what about you? What do you need?" she asked. *Please say someone young,* she silently prayed.

His mouth opened but no sound came out. "I don't know. No one has ever asked me that question before."

"And you've never given thought to the kind of woman you want to be with?"

"No, not ever."

"I can't fathom why none of your relationships have ever stuck," she said.

He cinched his arm around her neck in a loose chokehold. "Someone is aiming for a tickling again."

"Don't, I'll drown," she said, sounding somewhat panicked. The thought of drowning didn't bother her as much as having a convulsive laughing fit in front of his family.

She wondered if he guessed her thoughts because he gave her a squeeze and said, "We'll keep your tickle spots our little secret, then."

They talked for a long time, so long that the brothers drifted off one by one and left the tub.

"Maybe we should get out," she said after a while. "I'm pruning."

"Let me see," he commanded. He picked up her hand and inspected her wrinkled fingers. "If we stay in here much longer, you're going to look as old as me."

"You're not old," she blurted. Then, embarrassed by her earnest assessment, tried to backpedal. "I mean, you are old, but you don't look it."

"That's it, now you're going to get it," he said. He lunged for her and caught her around the waist, nuzzling his nose against her neck while she laughed convulsively. They were alone in the tub now, so she didn't mind as much, but the tickling was still torture.

"Stop it," she shrieked. Her attempts to fend him off were futile as he swung her arms up around his neck and pinned them in place. When he at last deemed she had been punished enough, he backed off, smiling as her laughter ebbed away. That was when they realized they were tightly pressed together with her arms around his neck and his arms around her waist.

They blinked at each other, either trying to scatter the droplets off their lashes or clear their heads, neither of them knew which. The sudden silence was oppressive as the now familiar tension settled between them and lingered. Haley watched his Adam's apple bob as he swallowed once and then again.

"Haley," he said softly.

"Hmm," she murmured.

"You want to go to a movie with me?"

The question, so out of the blue, caught her off guard and jogged her from her attraction-soaked haze. "What?"

"A movie," he repeated. He took a step back and dropped his hands. "You said you hadn't been to a movie in a long time. It could be fun. Don't you want to go?" he added when she continued to stare at him wordlessly.

"I can honestly say a movie was the last thing on my mind right now."

"Everyone likes movies," he blathered. He sidestepped her and hopped out of the tub. "I'm going to grab a quick shower. I'll catch you in the foyer, and we'll see a late show."

He walked into the house without a backward glance, leaving Haley staring at his hastily retreating backside.

CHAPTER 9

"You could have said no," Brent said when Haley yawned for the fifth time.

"I didn't think saying no to you was an option," she replied, fighting another yawn. They had made it to the movie theater in time for a nine o'clock showing. Haley was already tired and peeved because he had once again sidestepped the sizzling attraction between them, but she determined to have a good time. And then he chose a cartoon movie.

"Are you kidding me?" she asked as soon as she learned his selection.

He put his arm around her and ushered her into the theater, explaining as they walked. "One of my friends from college is an animator for this movie. Besides, it looks cute. Why are you angry?"

"I thought you were making this selection because it was age appropriate," she said.

He laughed and stepped aside so she could walk ahead of him into the aisle. "You're funny, Haley." They sat and he rested his arm on the back of her chair.

She studied the screen and vowed to try and stop analyzing his every move. If anyone could figure out Brent Honeywell, he would probably receive a Nobel Prize for his efforts.

After their initial rough start, they had fun. The movie was cute, but Haley was now exhausted. She was usually in bed asleep by ten on weeknights, and it was now almost midnight.

"Go to sleep, sugar," Brent urged.

"Brent," Haley said sleepily.

"Hmm," he said, not taking his eyes from the road.

"Please stop calling me sugar."

He turned to look at her then. "It offends you?" he asked incredulously.

She shook her head. "You call everyone sugar."

"Then why don't you like it?"

"Because you call everyone sugar," she repeated. She closed her eyes and rested her head on the window. Let him try to figure out her meaning for once.

In the morning, she woke up in the guest bed with no idea how she got there. Since she was still wearing her clothes, minus her shoes, she figured it was a safe bet that Brent had carried her, and she smiled.

He was so...everything. As she matured into adulthood, she had tried to tell herself her feelings for him were a crush, some sort of Freudian transference from her father to him. She needed a protector, and Brent stepped up to fill the spot. But this time together had settled her opinion on the matter. She was in love with Brent, really and truly Brent. With all his faults and foibles, he was still the best man she knew. How could there ever be anyone else for her?

She rose and took her time getting ready, dressing carefully for the day because Ivy was coming. The lone Honeywell sister was five years older than Haley, so they hadn't been friends. But Haley had distinct memories of watching her as she walked around town, so pristine and perfect. She had always seemed set apart somehow, but maybe that was only in comparison to her brothers. Whatever the reason, Haley was nervous about meeting her. Somehow she understood that Ivy was more perceptive and intuitive than her brothers. While they might like Haley simply because she was female, Ivy would have higher standards.

Brent was sitting at the breakfast table when she finally emerged from her room. "Morning, sug-" he cut himself off and gave her a sheepish smile. "Morning, Haley."

"Good morning," she said with a smile. Neither of them was aware of the way they froze and stared at each other, smiling, but everyone else realized, even the brothers who never noticed anything.

She sat beside him and put fruit on the plate that Sandy the housekeeper set before her.

"Better eat more than that," Brent said. "We've got a busy day ahead."

There was something in his gleeful tone Haley didn't understand, but maybe he was simply looking forward to a visit from his sister. Then his mother slammed her juice glass onto the table and gave a stern, sweeping look at her sons.

"I want you boys to be nice to your brother-in-law," she said.

"Mama, when are we anything but polite to the Yankee?" Darcy inquired.

She squeezed the bridge of her nose and let out an exaggerated sigh. "Please don't hurt him. Ivy would never forgive you."

"He'll be fine," they assured her.

Haley was puzzling over the exchange when she noted Sandy pause in front of Corliss and give him a look that could freeze a live coal. *What's that about,* she wondered. But the look was gone so quickly, she thought maybe she had imagined it. After all, what reason would a middle-aged housekeeper have to hate her employer? There was always the possibility that they had pranked her one time too many, but if that were the case, why would she single out Corliss? Why wouldn't she hate all the brothers? Maybe she did and Haley simply hadn't observed that side of her with anyone else.

While she was thinking about what had occurred, Brent added some protein to her plate and watched to make sure she ate it.

"Ready?" he asked when she was finished.

"I'm ready," she said. "What are we doing?"

"You'll see," was his cryptic reply. He stood and held her chair, pulling it back so she could ease away from the table, then he took her hand and led her outside. She noticed the other brothers were heading in the same direction.

They walked to one of the barns. Grant unrolled a set of blueprints. Brent let Haley go so he could surge forward with his brothers and gather around the blueprints. As a unit, they wordlessly studied the plans a few minutes before setting to work. Haley sat on a stump in the barn and watched while power tools and lumber emerged. With five capable men doing the building, whatever they were making took no time at all, especially because they worked as a fluid unit, as if they were communicating without words. She was reminded of twins she had seen on television who communicated with their own telepathic code, always in their own little world. It was the same with the brothers. As she sat there, ignored and forgotten, she cynically thought the brothers could probably coexist all by themselves without anyone else in the world.

On the other hand, it was nice that they were so close. And she wasn't totally ignored. Every once in a while, Brent would turn to smile or wink at her, as if assuring himself that she was still there and doing all right.

"You okay, sug-" he started to ask once. He stopped himself with an impatient shake of his head. "I really do use that word a lot, don't I?"

Haley smiled but didn't reply. As she sat and waited, she began to realize with dawning distress what was taking shape in front of her. They were building an elaborate trap. Lumber was being assembled and placed against the wall, camouflaged so artfully that it looked as if it had always been a part of the woodwork. A cable trailed down from the top of the wood to the floor where it made a circle, waiting for a foot to catch hold of. By the lever action they were now building, Haley could tell that whoever stepped in the circle on the floor would have his foot captured before being strung up to hang upside down until someone cut him down.

"You're making this for your brother-in-law," she said.

Brent shrugged. "We always prepare a sort of special greeting for him."

Haley reserved further comment for later. It was pointless to try and argue when he was with his brothers. She thought they almost formed a pack mentality, like wolves. However, she would try again to reason with him when they were alone.

Sooner than she would have thought possible, the task was completed and the trap was set. One brother scattered straw over the cable on the floor while the other brothers stood around admiring their handiwork.

"Think the cable will hold?" Everett asked.

"It'll hold," Grant assured him.

"He's a little thing," Darcy added. "It'll hold."

Haley felt even worse about the situation as she listened to them. Ivy's husband was apparently a small, weak man, and it infuriated her that the huge, muscled brothers preyed on him. For the first time since her arrival, she wasn't feeling very charitable about Brent, and it must have showed because he studied her with a wary expression as they left the barn.

"Something wrong?" he asked.

"I can't believe you do that to your brother-in-law," she said, pointing to the trap behind them.

"We're having a little fun with him," he said.

"Do you think he thinks it's fun? And what about Ivy? Do you think she enjoys having her husband tormented by her brothers? And, speaking of Ivy, what if she steps in that?" She jabbed her finger in the direction of the barn again. "What if she's holding the baby when she does so?"

"That's not going to happen," he said easily. "We arrange things to our specifications. It'll be him."

"Brent," she said, laying a hand on his arm to stop him from walking. "This isn't right. He's your family, the father of your niece, and you're being downright mean to him."

"Haley, this is what older brothers do. We look out for our sister.

The Yankee needs to know that we're always watching, and he'd better be on his toes where Ivy is concerned or we'll do much worse to him."

"So, let me get this straight, you stringing him up in a trap is supposed to teach him to be a good husband to your sister."

"Exactly," he said, relieved that she finally understood.

She put her hand to her head. "Brent, that's crazy. Why don't you try being nice to him and including him in your family?"

He shot her a dark look. "What kind of logic is that?"

"The kind where no one dangles from a trap. How do you know that thing is even safe?"

"Because Grant said so. He's an engineer," he explained. "His plans always work well."

That brought her up short. Grant was an engineer? What other secrets were the brothers hiding? Still, her irritation returned when she pictured the poor little brother-in-law, dangling helplessly from one of their traps. She was so intent on their discussion that she didn't notice the hole until she stepped in it. Then she pitched forward and landed hard on her hands and knees.

"Baby, are you okay?" Brent asked solicitously. He picked her up and set her on a nearby fence rail so he could make his inspection of her. He brushed grass and grit off her knees and looked at her palms.

"I think so," she replied, breathless from the hard fall.

He brushed at her hands, picked them up, and kissed her palms. "Better?" he asked.

She nodded, mesmerized by his tender ministrations. He seemed to be caught in the same trap because he moved closer and rested his hands on her hips. Her palms landed lightly on his shoulders.

"Is there anywhere else that hurts?" he asked. Was it her imagination, or did he glance at her lips?

Before she could summon a clever reply, there came the sound of a car winding down the long lane.

Haley and Brent remained rooted to their spots as the car came to a stop. Haley was almost bubbling over with curiosity about the brother-in-law, and she couldn't wait to see the baby, although she was still nervous about meeting Ivy. She waited, breathless, while first Ivy stepped out of the car, and then her husband.

By the Honeywells' description, she had expected to see a ninety eight pound weakling, possibly with glasses and leg braces, emerge from the driver's side of the car. Instead what she saw was a strapping cowboy wearing a Stetson. True, he was slightly shorter than the brothers, but he was still over six feet tall and every inch of him was muscle. Not only that, but he was smiling pleasantly, one deep dimple showing on the side of his face. He stood and stretched, watching his wife while she retrieved their baby from the back seat. Then his attention turned to Haley and Brent and he froze with a look of astonishment. Haley puzzled over that look, wondering if he had never seen Brent with a woman before.

"Come on," Brent said grudgingly. "Time to meet the relatives." He lifted Haley down and saw her grimace when she put weight on her foot. "Did you hurt you ankle?"

"I wrenched it a little; I think it's fine."

He bent and ran his hand over her ankle, feeling for injury. "I think you're right. Can you walk, or do you want me to carry you?"

Haley imagined her first meeting with Ivy while she was being carried in Brent's arms and cringed. "I'll definitely walk," she said. They strode over to Ivy and her husband who were standing by their car, waiting.

"Baby sister," Brent said cheerfully. He stepped forward and embraced Ivy, kissing her on both cheeks, being careful to avoid smashing the baby in her arms.

"Brent," she said lovingly, returning his hug as much as she could with one arm.

"Yankee," Brent said with a nod to the husband.

"Number One," the husband said, returning his nod. His smile didn't dim during the exchange, and, in fact, it deepened when his gaze settled on Haley. "And who do we have here?"

"This is Haley Griffin. She's a friend who is staying with us for a few days. Haley, this is my sister, Ivy, my niece, Jess, and her husband, the Yankee."

"Coy," the husband said, extending his hand. "And I have to tell you that I've been waiting a long time to meet you, Haley." His eyes sparkled as he shook her hand.

"What have you heard about Haley?" Brent asked suspiciously.

"Nothing," Coy said. "I've been waiting forever for this day. Praying for it, really."

"Well *I've* heard a lot about you," Ivy told Haley. "And I'm so glad to meet you." To Haley's surprise, Ivy stepped forward and gave her a one-armed hug.

"Here," Brent said. He stepped forward and took Jess from her mother's arms. "Let me hold my niece." He snuggled the infant close to his chest, burying his face against her neck to give her kisses that made her giggle with glee. "See, *she* likes being tickled," he threw over his shoulder to Haley.

Haley's cheeks warmed with a slight blush. "How old is she?" she asked.

"Four months," Ivy answered.

Haley stood on her toes to try and get a closer look at the baby. "She's beautiful," she exclaimed. She did look a lot like Ivy, with light blond hair and big blue eyes. The only piece of her father Ivy could see in her was a deep dimple on her right cheek.

"Want to hold her, sweetheart?" Brent asked, extending the baby toward her.

"Yes, I do," Haley said. "But I think your mother should probably see her first."

Brent nodded. "Good thinking. Let's get you inside to your grandma, Jess." He turned toward the house, Ivy following closely behind, chatting about the weather. Haley made sure they were facing forward before she grabbed Coy's sleeve and tugged. He hung back, shooting her a curious glance.

"The trap is in barn three, at the end, on the right hand side. There's a cable on the floor," she whispered.

Impossibly, his grin widened, the dimple now so deep his cheek appeared concave. "I knew you were good people, Haley," he whispered. "Better duck inside before they get suspicious." He went to the trunk to retrieve their luggage while Haley darted up the steps and into the house.

CHAPTER 10

As the day wore on, Haley began to realize that the feud between the Honeywell brothers and Coy King wasn't so much a matter of the weak versus the strong as it was a contest of equals. Coy was no one's idea of a weakling. His wit and humor were strong weapons against the brothers, none of whom could be accused of being perceptive or witty. They may have him outmaneuvered physically, but they were no match for his verbal parries. They knew it, and it made them all the angrier.

Coy had developed his own system of retaliation, first by never addressing the brothers by their names.

"I couldn't tell them apart for the longest time," he explained to Haley. "So I numbered them in order of age. Corliss really hates his number," he drawled.

Haley turned her head to laugh when she saw Corliss observing them with a frown. As the second brother in line, Coy had deemed him "Number Two."

Still, the Honeywells outnumbered Coy five to one, so Haley had no guilt about alerting him to their trap. And since he was on their turf, she figured he needed all the help he could get. And there was a secret small part of her that was rooting for him to win. She had known the Honeywells all her life and they always won. She liked them, but occasionally it would be good for them to get a little comeuppance.

"How long have you and Number One been together?" Coy asked.

Unfortunately, Brent overheard the question. "We're not together, Yankee. She's twenty. I'm her...she's my... We're friends."

Coy looked between Brent and Haley, studying the expressions on their faces, and then he smiled. Haley had the feeling that he understood everything in an instant—her feelings, Brent's refusal to see her as more than a child, and the ensuing tension those emotions caused.

"Oh," Coy said. "I see."

Brent's eyes narrowed, probably trying to figure out exactly what his brother-in-law saw. By the calculating gleam in Coy's eyes, Haley guessed he was about to have some fun. When he turned his attention to her, she knew she was correct.

"You should come to Montana sometime, Haley," Coy said. "Maybe I'm biased, but I believe it's the most beautiful place in the world. And if you're looking for a husband, there's no better place. My brothers and I are all happily settled, of course, but there are lots of available ranchers in the area who would be happy to..." He stopped speaking when Brent cut him off.

"She's not in the market for a husband," he snapped.

"Who says?" Haley interjected.

"You're only twenty," Brent said.

"Ivy and I were barely twenty two when we married," Coy pointed out. "And look how well that turned out."

Brent shook his head. "She's not going to Montana."

"Maybe I will," Haley mused. "I've always wanted to see it." That part was true; she had heard the state was majestic.

"You can stay with us," Coy offered. "We have plenty of room. And some of our ranch hands would be all too happy to..."

"Stop trying to pawn her off on men," Brent said. "Haley is not going to marry a Yankee. Someday, when she's older and ready, she'll marry someone from Kentucky like a good girl."

"Hear that, Haley?" Coy said. "Number One has it all worked out for you."

"Yes, he's very good at planning things out for me," Haley agreed.

Brent looked between them, not sure if they were being serious or making fun of him. "I know what's best."

"And if Haley doesn't agree to the plan, then what?" Coy asked.

"I'm working on it," Brent said with a pointed look at Haley.

"That's perfect, then," Coy said. "Montana can be her contingency plan."

"She doesn't need a contingency plan," Brent said, exasperated. "Stay out of it."

"I'm trying to help," Coy said innocently. "You know, how you help me so much in my relationship with your sister and my daughter. That kind of help."

Haley laughed and Brent put his arms around her, pinning them to her sides. "Don't encourage the Yankee, honey." He kissed her cheek, let her go, and walked away.

"One-upping him always feels a little too good," Coy said smugly. "But, seriously, Ivy and I would be happy to have you visit Montana anytime you can get away. I'm sure Ivy would love the chance to get to know you better."

She wondered why he thought Ivy would ever want to get to know her, but she didn't say so. "That's very kind of you, thank you." She smiled, and Brent returned holding baby Jess.

"Your turn," he said, shifting the sleeping baby into her arms.

"Oh," she gasped. "She's so precious."

"Isn't she, though?" Brent agreed. "If you did one thing right in your life, Yankee, it was her. Although you'll notice she looks mostly like my sister."

"Lucky her," Coy said, smiling down at his baby. "When are you going to get one of these, Number One?" he asked.

Brent shifted uncomfortably. "Now, that's a personal question."

Coy quirked an eyebrow. "This from the man who obtained a copy of my income tax return last year," he said.

"That was different," Brent said. He squirmed again and Coy's smiled deepened.

"Don't you want kids?" he pressed.

"Of course I do," Brent said.

"Then what's holding you back?" Coy asked.

"You need a wife before you can make babies," Brent said.

"Then get a wife. You have a good, solid plan for Haley. What's your plan?" Not waiting for him to answer, Coy turned to Haley. "What about you, Haley? You want kids don't you?"

"I love kids," Haley said. "I would like to have them as soon as I get married. Although, I'm not sure how Brent would feel about that."

"Why would that be any of my concern?" Brent asked. He tugged at his collar and cleared his throat, his eyes darting for an escape.

"Well, you seem to have a timeline planned out for me. I wondered when I'm allowed to have kids," Haley said.

"You, uh, need to finish college, and then get married, so, uh, I would say sometime in your mid-twenties."

"But that's only a few years away," she pointed out. "That means I need to meet the right man and get married now. I should go call Tyler."

"Who's Tyler?" Coy asked, clearly enjoying himself.

"Oh, Tyler and I have been dating off and on since high school. We've never been very serious, but Brent has been making me rethink some things. It *would* be nice to marry someone from Kentucky, and Tyler and I have so much history together."

That got Brent's attention. He stopped staring around the room and scowled at Haley. "I haven't even met the boy."

"So, that's part of your plan? You have to approve him?" Coy interjected.

"Of course I have to approve him," Brent said. "She can't marry just anybody."

"But what if she does?" Coy asked. "What if you meet the guy, don't like him, but she marries him anyway? Her husband would never let her see you again. I know I wouldn't if some other man disapproved of me for Ivy. Unless he was family and I had no choice in the matter," he added dryly.

"Haley wouldn't marry someone I don't approve of. Would you, Haley?" He looked at her then with something like vulnerability, and Haley lost the heart to continue to tease him.

"Is there anyone you would approve of for me, Brent?" she asked seriously.

"No," he said, equally as serious.

"Then what am I supposed to do?" she asked. "Who am I supposed to marry?"

"How about one of your brothers?" Coy suggested. "Certainly a Honeywell is good enough for her."

"They're all too old," Brent said dismissively.

"Well then it seems to me there are two options on the table: either Haley can remain single and miserable because there's no one good enough for her, or she can marry someone who is good enough for her and be happy, despite the fact that he might be too old for her. So which is better, Number One? For Haley to be alone, or for her to be with someone who makes her happy, despite the age difference?" He let the words hang, not staying nearby to hear Brent's answer.

Haley was deeply curious about Brent's answer, but he didn't give one. "Meddling Yankee," he mumbled, watching Coy's retreating backside with a mutinous frown. "Now is a good time to take him out to the barn."

Since Haley knew a trip to the barn would result in the brothers' plan being foiled, and therefore a further bad mood for Brent, she hastened to put him off. "That can wait," she said soothingly. "Let's sit down and you can admire your beautiful niece with me."

They found a seat on one of the long sofas in the living room. Brent put his arm around her, presumably so he could see the baby, although he didn't look at the baby; he looked at Haley. She was a soft, warm, and feminine person, and he liked that about her. The baby looked so natural in her arms, he could almost believe the baby was hers. If she were old enough to be married and have kids, which she wasn't, he sternly reminded himself. She was off limits to anyone until she got a degree. Then she could…what?

Right now his priority was sending her to college, but what happened after? What if she married the boy she had been dating since high school? What if he was horrible—stupid, a drunk, disrespectful, or anything else that would doom a marriage and hurt Haley? How could Brent stand by and watch her with someone who might hurt her? And what about him? What would happen to their friendship when he someday married? No wife in her right mind would want her husband looking after a young girl, especially not one as pretty, sweet, smart, and lovely as Haley. That was a recipe for disaster. So what were they to do?

If he really cared about her as much as he thought he did, then he wanted her to be happy. He wanted the best for her. In his mind, there was only one thing to be done.

"I want to meet your boyfriend," he blurted, so abruptly that baby Jess woke and began to wail.

CHAPTER 11

"May I state for the record one more time that this is a really bad idea?" Haley said. She and Brent were in his truck, driving to meet Tyler at the same bistro Brent had taken her to a couple of days ago. "You should be spending time with your sister."

"I want to get this over with before it goes any further," he said. Noting the way he leaned forward, gripping the steering wheel, she wondered exactly what he meant.

"You're going to be nice to him, aren't you?" she asked.

"When am I ever not nice?" he asked with a menacing scowl.

"Why are you doing this?"

"I want to make sure he's a good guy, someone I approve of."

"I already told you he's a good guy, and I have my doubts you'll approve of anyone."

"I'm trying to keep an open mind for your sake," he said. "I don't want you to end up alone."

She turned toward the window and rolled her eyes. How was it that he had taken some of what Coy said to heart, yet missed the point entirely? Was he now going to try and set her up with other men in order to make sure she didn't die alone?

"Brent, you know that when it comes down to it, who I marry is my decision."

"Be reasonable, Haley," he said.

"That's strange; I didn't know that word was in your vocabulary."

He reached over to squeeze her knee. "You be good," he commanded.

"Me?" she said, pointing to her chest. "You be good. Tyler is a nice guy, and I don't want you scaring him."

"If he's a nice guy, then he'll have no reason to worry," he said, but Haley was still worried. Tyler *was* a nice guy, and he didn't deserve any torture Brent might put him through. And he was coming into this meeting blind. Not knowing how to describe her relationship with Brent, she hadn't tried. She had simply asked Tyler to meet them for lunch. And Tyler, being Tyler, hadn't asked any questions.

They arrived at the restaurant first.

"He's late," Brent said.

She pressed her index finger lightly to his lips. "You promised to be good."

In answer, he kissed her fingertip and winked.

"Hales!" Tyler called as soon as he stepped into the entryway and spotted her.

"Hey!" she said with the same amount of enthusiasm. She stood and they embraced as soon as he reached her table. Unlike some of their peers in high school who seemed to thrive on angst and drama, Tyler and Haley had always had a fun, healthy relationship. Haley secretly wondered if Brent was the reason. She was so busy mooning over him that she lacked the emotional energy to invest in anyone else. Or maybe Tyler was the cause of their lackadaisical relationship. If they lived near the ocean, he would definitely be a surfer with his shaggy blond hair, blue/green eyes, and easygoing attitude.

"I'm so glad you called," he said. He gave her an extra squeeze and kissed her cheek. "I've missed you."

Except for smiling at him, Haley didn't reply. The knife of guilt twisted in her gut both at his words and his happy expression. She liked Tyler, but when she wasn't with him, she didn't think about him much.

"Tyler, this is Brent Honeywell."

"Mr. Honeywell," Tyler said, politely extending his hand.

Haley choked back a laugh and Brent poked her under the table. "How do you do, Tyler," he said with formal politeness. Haley was relieved to note that he didn't try to one up Tyler's handshake by crushing his hand.

Tyler sat and studied the menu while Brent studied him.

"Are you in college, Tyler?" he asked.

"Yes, sir," Tyler said, peering over the top of his menu before returning his attention to the cheeseburger selection.

"What's your major?"

"Business administration."

"That's a good major," Brent said approvingly. "What do you plan to do with it?"

Realizing he wasn't going to be able to finish his selection, Tyler finally set the menu aside and gave Brent his full attention. "I dunno. My dad talked me into it. I guess I'll figure something out after I graduate. Everyone assures me it's a good major that covers all the bases."

"Hmm," Brent said.

Tyler stared at him, puzzling over his disapproving tone. He turned his attention to Haley and smiled. "It's good to see you, Hales. Hey, Avery is having a party tomorrow. You should totally go with me."

"That sounds great, Tyler, but I'm sort of staying with the Honeywells all week."

Tyler looked back and forth between them, most likely trying to figure out their relationship.

Don't try, Haley wanted to tell him. *Or at least if you get it figured out, let me know what it is.* "You see, Brent and I are sort of..." She trailed off and looked helplessly at Brent.

Tyler sat up a little straighter, his smile slipping slightly. "Sort of what?" His incredulous tone told her he didn't think she meant romance, but had no idea what she could be talking about.

"Friends. We're friends," Brent said.

"Were you and Haley's dad friends from high school or something?" he asked.

Brent and Haley both winced slightly at the mention of her father. "No, Brent never knew my father," Haley said quietly. "And he's apparently much younger than you think. He's only thirty-two."

"Oh," Tyler said. Haley knew him well enough to understand that he was thinking thirty-two was still old.

The waitress arrived to take their orders. Brent told Tyler the meal was his treat and urged him to order the steak. Tyler's face lit like he had won the lottery, and Haley smiled. Since he was putting himself through college, she knew his funds were tight. That was one of the reasons they rarely went out on dates.

"Do you have siblings?" Brent asked the question abruptly, as if they had been in mid-conversation already.

"I have a brother and a sister," Tyler said uncertainly.

"What is your birth order?" Brent asked. Haley half expected him to whip out a pad and paper to write down his observations.

"I'm in the middle."

Brent nodded. "That's good. Middle kids are more pliable."

Tyler shot Haley a look. She shrugged helplessly.

"Do you have a job?" Brent demanded.

"I have two part-time jobs," Tyler replied. He shifted uncomfortably. "Is that what this is about? Is this an interview?"

"Of sorts," Brent replied with a vague wave of his hand. "Do these places you work perform routine drug tests?" he added.

"Brent," Haley exclaimed.

Brent ignored her and focused on Tyler so hard that Tyler squirmed again. "No, but I don't do drugs, so it doesn't really matter."

Brent nodded. "Good. That's good."

The questions continued until the food arrived and then came to an end. Haley naively thought they were over forever, but as soon as Brent finished his food he began again, asking Tyler everything from his financial strategy to which baseball team was his favorite.

Tyler answered them all, but his tone became warier and warier as the evening wore on. He kept darting questioning looks at Haley who had no help to offer. "Sorry," she mouthed more than once.

At last Brent seemed to be satisfied, or maybe he simply ran out of questions. Whatever the case, he lightly slapped his palm on the table and said, "Okay, I've heard enough."

Tyler blinked in confusion. "Did I get a job or something?"

Now it was Brent's turn to look confused. "Do you want a job?"

"I thought your family was hiring."

"We are. The job involves a lot of heavy lifting. Does that suit you?"

"Sure," Tyler said, his easy smile returning.

"Okay, then. The job is yours. I'll talk to my father, and have his secretary give you a call. I'll get the truck and meet you outside, Haley." He scooted from the booth and left them.

Tyler and Haley watched him walk away before turning to each other.

"That was one of the weirdest nights of my life," Tyler whispered.

"I'm sorry," Haley said. She reached over the table to clasp his hand and give it a squeeze.

"What was that?" he asked. "And don't say it was about a job because I know better."

"Brent's protective of me, I guess."

"Why? I had no idea you even knew him, and now you're staying at his house."

"It's a long story," she said. "I've known him for a long time, since I was five."

"Since your dad died," Tyler said slowly. He was putting the pieces together in his head. "You said a teenager was driving the other car that hit you guys. Was it him?" He nodded his head toward the exit.

Haley nodded.

"Whoa, that's heavy, Haley. How can you stand to be around the guy who killed your dad?"

"He didn't kill my dad," she said vehemently. "The accident was my dad's fault."

"Still," Tyler said. "Doesn't being near him make all the bad memories surface?"

"No," Haley said. "He's done his best to erase any bad memories from that day." She bit her lip, thinking of how hard Brent had worked to try and make up for that day when, in reality, he didn't owe her anything. She had always thought he did nice things for her because they had forged some sort of bond that day, but what if he remained in her life out of misplaced guilt?

"Whatever the reason, you should be careful," Tyler said. "Those Honeywells are…well, you know."

"They're not," she said, trying hard not to make her tone defensive. "I agree they can be a little overwhelming at times, but they're all very kind and gentle. You have to get to know them."

"That's like saying you have to get to know a grizzly bear before you can judge it for eating people," he said. Then he smiled his usual, sunny smile and stood. He clasped her hand and used it to pull her up to stand in front of him. "I've really missed you, Hales. Let's do something as soon as you're done with the Honeywells."

I'll never be done with them, she thought. Out loud she said, "I'd like that, Tyler. We've both been so crazy lately, it would be great to have some fun."

He pulled her into a tight hug and kissed the top of her head. "You go on out. I think I'll stay here until he's gone," Tyler said. He cast a worried glance toward the door.

"He's really very nice," Haley assured him.

"If you say so," Tyler said. "All the same, I'll wait here a few minutes." He sat back down and waved at her as she walked away.

Brent met her at the door and boosted her into his truck. They didn't talk for the first few minutes, but it was an easy silence.

"I would like to point out that I was perfectly nice to him," Brent said at last.

"I suppose that depends on your definition of nice," Haley said. "You didn't physically assault him, but you did batter him with about a thousand questions."

"What's a few questions? Besides, I got the answer I was looking for."

Since he didn't come right out and say it, she tried to draw it out of him. "He's a nice guy, isn't he?"

"He is. I didn't realize he was your senior prom date. I already vetted him when he was in high school, but it's good to know he's still on the right track."

She decided to set aside the fact that he had stalked her dates in high school, at least for the moment. "Are you telling me you approve of him for me?"

He snorted. "No way."

She gritted her teeth together. "Why not?"

"Because he's way too young for you," Brent said. Then he turned on the radio as if the conversation was over.

CHAPTER 12

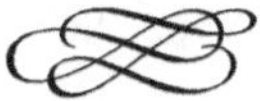

$\mathcal{H}$aley reached forward, straining against her seatbelt, and snapped off the radio. "What?" she said. Her voice was evenly controlled, betraying none of her inner frustration.

"He's too young for you," Brent repeated. His tone was nonchalant. They might have been discussing the weather instead of her boyfriend and her future.

"What?" she repeated. When he glanced at her, she continued. "What do you mean he's too young for me? He's three months older."

"I'm not talking about physical age. I'm talking about maturity. Tyler's a nice kid, but that's it: he's a kid. He has no idea what he wants to do with his life, and he still likes to party with his friends."

"And why is any of that bad?" she asked.

"It's not bad, it's just not for you. You're very mature for your age. You need someone older, someone with direction, someone more settled."

This time she couldn't keep the cap on her emotions. She actually growled at him, something she had never done before.

"What?" he asked innocently. "I thought you would be happy I think he's a nice kid. For high school, he was a good choice for you.

But high school is over, and it's time to start thinking about your future."

She pressed her palms over her ears. "Stop talking. Stop talking before I scream."

"What?" he asked again. "What's wrong with you?"

She shook her head furiously. Tears of frustration pricked her eyes, and she squeezed them tightly closed. They finished the remainder of their drive in silence. When they arrived at the Honeywell farm, she tried to dart into the house, but he was faster. He caught her, pinning her between him and the truck.

"Haley, I know I can be overbearing at times," he said. He framed her face with his hands and used his thumbs to wipe the tears sparkling on her lashes. "But I always mean well. You believe that, don't you?"

She searched his earnest expression and came to the conclusion that he truly had no idea why she was upset with him. How could someone go through thirty two years of life and remain so clueless? Suddenly it was all too much for Haley. She burst into tears and pressed her face to his chest.

"Ah, Haley, don't cry," he said urgently. His arms eased around her and held her close. His head rested gently on hers. "I'm sorry you think I was too tough on your boyfriend. I'll apologize to him if it will help."

She couldn't take hearing him apologize for the wrong thing anymore. She slipped her hand up and pressed it against his lips. "Don't," she choked. Had she misread the chemistry between them? Did Brent truly see her as his little sister or something equally as innocuous? How humiliating, if that were the case.

Brent was becoming more desperate by the second. He had no idea what was wrong with her and no idea how to fix her. Apologizing didn't help. What was he to do? "Please stop crying," he begged. "Tell me what's wrong, and I'll fix it." His lips skimmed her temple as he spoke, and Haley's tears began to dry as an idea occurred to her.

What if she simply asked him to kiss her? Then she would know once and for all if there was any chemistry between them or if she had imagined the whole thing. She lifted her face and almost smiled at the intense worry that was in his expression. "Brent," she said, her voice still wobbly from emotion.

"What is it, baby?" he asked. He pushed her hair off her face, pulling the strands off her wet cheek.

"Will you…" she began and then stopped. She couldn't do it. She couldn't make herself that vulnerable, at least not where Brent Honeywell was concerned. What if he rejected her? She truly believed she might die if that happened.

"Will I what? I'll do anything, Haley, you know I will," he said. "All you have to do is ask."

Will you kiss me? Will you love me the way I love you? Will you promise me forever? "Will you give me a minute before we go into the house? I don't want anyone to know I've been crying."

"Sure," he said eagerly, glad the request was something simple that he could grant right away. "Want to look in the mirror?" He lifted her up so she could fix her face in the mirror attached to the visor. When she finished, he was leaning against the truck door watching her with a smile.

"Did I tell you you're a beauty, Haley? Because you are."

She smiled, her cheeks pinking slightly at the compliment, and then she decided to return it. "Did I tell you you're handsome, Brent? Because you are."

He stood up quickly and snapped his dangling mouth closed, clearing his throat. "We, uh, should probably get inside if you're ready."

Haley chuckled, knowing she had flustered him. There was something especially amusing about seeing such an unflappable man ruffled. She could have pressed the issue and made him squirm, but she didn't. Instead, she hopped on his back and kissed his cheek.

"I'm ready," she said.

"Hold on," he said. He jogged to the house, bouncing her wildly on his back. She secretly wondered if he was simply trying to burn off the rush of adrenaline her compliment and his ensuing embarrassment had caused.

He stopped at the door and offered her a hand to help her hop off. She decided to push the envelope a little further by whispering in his ear. "I think you're pretty cute, Brent."

She should have known better than to think she would be able to fluster him a second time. Instead of helping her down, he grasped her hand and used it to hold her in place as he turned and pinned her against the house.

"You do?" he asked. "You want to know something? That's mutual. You're about the cutest thing I've ever seen." The tension between them was immediate and thick, all traces of humor quickly evaporated.

Haley swallowed hard, trying to hold her own, trying not to let his one-upmanship intimidate her. "What are you going to do about it?" she asked.

"That's a good question," he said slowly. His eyes fell to her lips and lingered. She wondered if he was having some sort of internal debate. If it had been Tyler or anyone else, she would have tipped her head up, met his lips, and kissed him. But Brent wasn't the sort of man who would appreciate having the woman make the first move. So she waited an agonizingly long minute for him to speak again.

"I suppose I'll have to give you to Grant."

"What?"

He let her go and took a step back. "Grant, you know, my youngest brother. I still think twenty-six is a little too old for you, but you're much more mature than most twenty-year-olds. Probably because you've been taking care of yourself for so long." If she didn't know better, she might think he was babbling nervously.

"What?" she repeated again. She was saying that a lot lately and he never seemed to get that she didn't mean she hadn't heard him; she meant she didn't understand him. But how could she when what he was saying was so insane? "What do you mean you're *giving* me to your brother? Do you have any idea how horrible and archaic that sounds?"

"Obviously I didn't mean it in a bad way," he said.

"Oh, obviously," she said sarcastically.

"I simply meant that I am revising my earlier opinion. Grant's not too old for you."

"So Grant's not too old for me, but you are," she said. Finally saying the words that hung between them felt good.

"Be serious, Haley," he said.

"You be serious, Brent. I am not a filly to be passed off to one of your brothers, and if you don't know that, then you're not the man I thought you were." With her head held high, she stalked past him, into the house, and down the hall to her bedroom. Once she was finally safe in the privacy of her room, she threw herself on the bed and cried herself to sleep.

The next morning, Haley dreaded leaving her room, but she needn't have worried; Brent was nowhere around.

"I told Brent I wanted to kidnap you for the day and have some girl time," Ivy explained. "I thought we could spend some time at the spa if you don't mind. Mom is going to watch Jess for me."

"I don't mind," Haley said--an understatement if she'd ever made one. She had never been to a spa and was dying for the experience.

They were in the middle of breakfast when Corliss came in and sat down at the table, smiling at them. Sandy, the housekeeper, came in, took one look at Corliss, and walked back out of the room with a scowl.

Corliss sighed and stood to retrieve his own breakfast from the sideboard. "Think I'll eat outside," he muttered through his jaw wires.

Ivy waited to speak until she watched him go, then she tossed a furtive look toward the kitchen. "Did you see that?" she whispered to Haley.

Haley nodded. "That's the second time I've noticed something like that," she whispered. "She really doesn't like him, does she?"

"No. Corliss used to date her daughter, Allie. Something happened, no one knows what, and Allie went away. Sandy blames Corliss."

Haley whistled softly. "That's awful," she said, puzzling over what might have made the girl go away. "Were they serious?"

Ivy shrugged. "With my brothers who can tell? They never talk to me about stuff like that. I'm not even sure they tell each other. They all have the emotional maturity of newborns."

Haley would have laughed if her own experience with Brent wasn't so fresh in her mind. Instead she nodded in solemn agreement. Ivy laughed, though.

"I guess you'd know about that firsthand," she said. "Although Brent seems like a different person when he's with you. I've never seen him so open or soft before."

"Open?" Haley repeated incredulously. "You think he's open with me?"

"Compared to what he usually is, I'd say he's the Grand Canyon where you're concerned." She smiled. "It's nice to see one of my brothers in love. And Coy is beside himself with glee. He's been waiting for this day for four years since we got together. I think he feels the need for a little retribution." She noted Haley's stricken expression and hastened to add, "But don't worry; I won't let him snag you in his twisted payback schemes."

That wasn't why Haley was speechless, though. It was something else in Ivy's statement that shocked her, numbing her brain. "You think he's in love with me?" By the time she was able to speak the words, the conversation was long over, but Ivy seemed to have no trouble picking it up again.

"Of course he is; it's so obvious. It's written all over his face. Even the rest of my brothers can see it, and they never see anything."

"Maybe one of them could tell Brent," Haley muttered.

Ivy gave her a sympathetic smile. "He'll come around," she said. "Be patient. It takes longer with him, but I have a feeling when he finally realizes he's in love with you, he won't do anything halfway." She paused and bit her lip. "So I guess you'd better be ready for forever with him, because when he goes, it's going to be like a redwood toppling."

"I'm ready," Haley said with no hesitation. There was no one else for her but Brent, and she knew it. "I have no doubts," she added, but she wasn't sure if that was true. She didn't doubt herself, but despite

Ivy's comforting words, she doubted Brent. "Sometimes I think he sees me as a little sister," she confessed.

"I think he used to, and that's what's adding to his confusion. Brent doesn't accept change easily, even in himself. For so long he had you categorized as a little girl he looked after. It's hard for him to make the mental and emotional transition and accept the fact that you're a woman and he's in love with you."

Haley nodded, appreciating the insight into Brent's thought process. Sometimes she was so uncertain of him. But Ivy was his sister; she knew him as well as anyone could, didn't she? If she said he loved her, then that must mean he loved her. Why, then, was there still a kernel of doubt in Haley's mind?

"Are you ready for the spa?" Ivy asked, cajoling her our of her morose mood.

"Definitely," Haley said. She was thankful for the opportunity to shove everything from her mind and simply relax.

Ivy must have been thinking the same thing. "This is such a treat for me, Haley. Thanks for coming. There aren't any spas where we live in Montana, so I usually try to go to one when I come to Kentucky. But I didn't want to go alone, and Mom couldn't come because she's watching Jess. Plus this will give us a chance to get to know each other. I've always been curious about you."

"Why?" Haley asked.

"Because of the way Brent talked about you."

"How did he talk about me?" she asked.

"Soft." Ivy paused. "I have to confess that when I was much younger, I was a little jealous of you. He was always so hard on me, and when he talked about you, his tone was almost reverential."

"Brent has always been amazing to me. But you should hear the way he talks about you, like you're a precious treasure."

Ivy raised an eyebrow at her.

"I'm serious," Haley said. "I think it was really hard on him to let you go when you got married."

"He made that abundantly clear," Ivy said dryly, causing Haley to laugh. "Coy is a saint."

"He seems like a very nice guy, and he also seems to love you very much."

Ivy smiled fondly. "There's nothing better than a good marriage," she said happily.

Haley's answering smile was melancholy. She was happy for Ivy, of course, but had her doubts that things would ever work out for her. Thankfully before she could descend fully into despair, they arrived at the spa. She intended simply to get a manicure because it was what she could afford, but Ivy not only insisted on paying; she insisted that Haley have the total spa treatment.

After a manicure, pedicure, massage, facial, brow wax, hair conditioning treatment, and makeup session, the women returned home feeling almost brand new and deeply relaxed. That was why when Brent greeted her with a bouquet of flowers held over his face, she had no idea why he seemed almost afraid of her.

"You still mad at me?" he asked.

The conversation from the previous evening came rushing back, but no lingering anger came with it. "No," she said.

He put down the flowers, held out his arms, and she walked into them, enjoying his snug embrace. "For whatever I did, I'm sorry," he said.

She almost smiled. He was contrite and clueless, an endearing combination in a man. "I don't want you to pass me off to one of your brothers," she tried to explain.

"Okay," he quickly agreed. "I don't think I could anyway. I would get upset with him if he didn't treat you the way I want you to be treated." He rested his head on hers. "I guess I'll have to keep looking for someone."

She eased away from him and looked up. He winced at the hurt in her expression. "No. Don't look for anyone. I don't want you setting me up with anyone."

"Okay," he said, clearly confused.

"Promise?" she said.

"I promise," he said.

Satisfied, she nodded once and rested her head on his chest again.

His heart thumped under her ear and the sound, along with his solid mass, was intensely comforting.

"What are we going to do about it?" he asked.

Now it was her turn to be confused. "What?"

"You and your future. I don't want you to be alone like the Yankee said."

"There are worse things than being alone," she said. *For instance, you could be in love with someone who can't seem to see past the end of his nose.*

"Not for you. You deserve to be with someone special."

She squinched her eyes tightly shut. "Brent, can we agree my love life is off limits?"

"All right," he said after a pause. There was another comfortable lull between them. They swayed slightly together, almost like they were dancing to unheard music, and then he spoke again. "I hate to shatter this peaceful moment with another sour topic, but your mother's boyfriend called while you were away."

"He called here?" She felt intensely embarrassed by the revelation. Obviously he had caught wind of her stay and thought he could wrangle some investment money out of the Honeywells.

"We're having dinner with him and your mother tomorrow night."

She pulled back to look at him again. "Brent, no. You know he wants your money."

"I know," he said. "And he and I are going to have a little talk about that. He's going to leave you alone."

"He doesn't bother me," she said.

"I still don't like it. He sounds like a predator."

"He's a financial planner, and he's a bit seedy. That's all there is to it. Please, I don't want to do this." Haley thought she might die of humiliation if her mother's boyfriend made a pitch to Brent for his money. She hated the thought of anyone connected with her trying to fleece them for cash.

"You should see your mother," Brent said gently.

"My mother doesn't want to see me. You'll notice the meeting wasn't her idea."

"Still, mothers and daughters shouldn't stay apart so long."

Haley sighed. Brent had an idealized version of her mother in his head because his mother was the ideal. Mrs. Honeywell was a loving and involved mother who could never fathom going a year without seeing one of her children, especially when they lived in the same town.

"I know you don't want to do this," Brent said soothingly. "But I'll feel better if we get this taken care of. I want to meet them to know what we're dealing with."

"Evenings spent with my mother are notoriously uncomfortable," Haley said.

"I won't let it be uncomfortable," Brent said. "We'll do this together."

The corner of Haley's mouth quirked into a smile. If they did everything together, she was sure there was nothing they couldn't handle.

Ivy opened the front door and poked her head around. "It's such a nice night and Haley and I look too good to be kept indoors. Y'all want to go for a walk?"

"Sure thing, sugar," Brent answered for both of them, belatedly looking to Haley for approval. She gave a slight nod, and he smiled. Coy joined them on the porch. He and Ivy took the lead, walking hand in hand.

Brent reached over and clasped Haley's hand, twining their fingers together. "I'm following the leader," he said with a wink. The sun was beginning to set, sinking large and round over the horizon. The air was brisk without being cold. The autumnal scent of drying leaves hung heavy in the breeze. Haley smiled as they walked and took in the beauty of the farm; she wasn't sure she had ever felt so peaceful.

Brent let go her hand and slid his arm around her shoulder, drawing her slightly closer so he could whisper in her ear. "What's your favorite season?"

She looked up at him with a considering smile. "It's always whatever season we're in the middle of. I guess I'm wishy-washy that way."

"Or maybe you're good at living in the moment," he said, giving her shoulders a squeeze.

"What's your favorite?" he asked.

"Spring," he answered without hesitation. "I always look forward to seeing all the new foals, and I love the way the hardy perennials pop their heads up even though the ground is still frozen and crusted with snow. You have to admire something so indomitable."

She slipped her arm around his waist, giving him a squeeze. She didn't realize they had entered the barn until they stopped short in front of a stall. "This is my favorite barn," Ivy commented, sounding nostalgic.

"It is pretty," Coy agreed.

Brent said nothing, although he threw a glance over his shoulder. Haley tried not to stare at the trap in the corner. She sensed some sort of confrontation in the works, and she was anxious that her traitorous role would be revealed.

"What is that?" Ivy said abruptly.

"What?" Brent said. He sounded anxious.

"Over there in the corner. It's like one of those panels is disturbed. I've never noticed before." She turned to Brent with a smile. "Do you think it could be a secret passage? Dad told me once he thought there might be secret passages in some of these barns or in the house."

"It's not a secret passage, baby," Brent said. He clasped her hand and tried to tug her from the barn. "Let's go back inside. Isn't it about Jess's bedtime?"

"She's with Corliss," Ivy said absently. She shook off Brent and headed toward the trap in the corner.

"Ivy, come back here," Brent said. "That's not a secret panel." He ran his hand through his hair, disheveling it. As Ivy was about to step in the trap, he leapt forward and put his foot in the trap, his body swinging through the air in a wide arc.

Coy gasped in mock horror. "A trap. Now how did that get there?" He walked forward and stood in front of Brent who dangled like a fish on a hook. Coy made a tsking sound. "You know, Number One, if I believed in karma, I might say you're finally getting what's been coming to you."

Brent tucked his shirt in his pants to stop it from flopping over his head. "All right, Yankee, you've had your fun. Are you going to get me down?"

Coy studied the trap. "I don't know," he said slowly. "This looks mighty complicated. I think you need a real man to operate it. I'll go and try to track down one of your brothers."

He turned and loped cheerfully away. Ivy remained, hands on hips, shaking her head at Brent. "Shame on you, big brother, for trying to hurt my husband."

"It doesn't hurt," Brent said. "Are you going to let him get away with leaving me here?"

"What do you think?" she asked.

"I think if you walk out that door, you're drawing a line in the sand, baby sister."

"That line was drawn the day I got married." She leaned down to kiss his chin, then followed Coy out of the barn. That left Haley, trying hard not to look guilty. She must not have succeeded because Brent crossed his arms over his chest and studied her through narrowed eyes, upside down.

"I find it highly suspicious that the Yankee somehow found our trap. I think someone tipped him off, but surely not you, Haley. Please tell me it wasn't my girl."

It was hard to feel the full impact of his emotional manipulation when he was swinging back and forth, his face getting redder by the second. "I'll get you down if you tell me how," she said.

"I'm not sure you want me to get down from here because when I do, you're going to get it."

"Now Brent," she said nervously, "it was five against one. He needed an edge."

"He has an edge," he said. "He has Ivy."

She realized then that it wasn't all big-brotherly bluster on his part; it truly pained him to see Ivy gone and living so far away. She went forward and sat beneath him, cradling his head in her lap to stop him from swinging. "You're always going to be Ivy's big brother, and no one can take that away, not even her husband. But you want her to be happy, and she's happy. You should stop fighting against that, or you really will lose her. She adores you. Let her."

He was silent a minute, considering, and then he smiled. "You're even pretty upside down, you know that."

She smiled, smoothing her thumbs over his cheeks. When they moved to caress his lips, he sucked in a breath. "Haley," he said shakily, but she ignored him. She finally had him where she wanted him, pinned down like a struggling butterfly. This was her chance. She leaned forward, closing the gap between them, when she heard the brothers troop into the other end of the barn.

"How on earth did that happen?" Darcy said.

"It worked," Grant said, sounding relieved.

Everett, the tallest, reached up without a ladder, hit a switch, and sent Brent plummeting to the earth. Thankfully he was prepared and had put his hands down, so that he sprang lightly to his feet. The next second he was stalking toward Haley.

"Better run, little girl."

"I thought we talked it out," she said.

"Doesn't mean you're not getting punished," he replied.

Squealing, she turned and darted for the door, but it was too late. He caught her and tickled her until she was crying with laughter and begging for mercy, and then he let her go.

CHAPTER 13

Haley was more nervous about the dinner with her mother than she had been about anything in a long time. She had grown used to her mother's indifference, but that didn't mean it ever stopped hurting. Seeing her again always had the unsavory effect of reopening the old wound. Life was easier for both of them if they went their separate ways.

"You're certainly pushing me to my limits this week," Haley said as she and Brent drove to the restaurant in Lexington.

Brent frowned. "That's not what this week is about."

"Then what is it about?" She felt almost like she was spoiling for a fight with him. At least if they argued it would give her a channel for her restless emotions.

"It's about tying up the loose ends of your life and making sure you're doing well. I've neglected you these two years, and for that I'm sorry. This is my way of making amends."

"You don't need to make amends, Brent. You don't need to take care of me. I'm not your responsibility."

He quirked an eyebrow in her direction, but otherwise didn't respond.

"It's like arguing with a brick wall sometimes," she muttered.

"We're not arguing," he insisted. "You would know if we were arguing."

She shuddered, realizing the truth of his statement. He was remarkably even-tempered. Except for his initial outburst in the restaurant, he hadn't been angry with her all week. But she knew if he ever was angry at her, she would know it. As a unit, the Honeywell brothers had legendary tempers, but usually they were only provoked by injustice. Everyone knew better than to mistreat a horse anywhere nearby because nothing made them angrier than seeing an animal mistreated.

Since Brent wasn't cooperating by giving her the argument she needed, she turned her attention to the window, fidgeting restlessly in her seat until he reached over and placed a hand on her knee.

"Haley, it's going to be okay," he assured her.

She swallowed hard as a sudden lump of emotion lodged in her throat. "You don't know what it's like with her." And she didn't want him to know. She didn't want him to bear witness to her mother's lack of maternal devotion. Though she knew it wasn't rational, Haley had come to feel a large portion of shame over her mother's disinterest. What was wrong with her that her own mother didn't want her? Now Brent, the person whose opinion meant the most in the world, was about to see for himself the truth of their relationship. Would he also blame Haley? How could he love her when her own mother didn't?

They pulled into the restaurant parking lot. He turned off the truck, but made no move to get out. Instead, he clicked off his seatbelt, then reached over to unclasp hers. He slid across the seat and put his hands on her shoulders.

"You are beautiful, lovely, intelligent, warm, and caring. I think you're the best person I know, and if your mother doesn't see that, then it's her loss. How you turned out well in spite of her indifference is a mystery, but I'm glad you did. I know this night is going to be painful for you, but I didn't drag you here to put you through an ordeal. I brought you here because I want them to know you're not alone. You're under my protection, and they can't hurt you. Do you understand?"

No, she didn't understand. She didn't understand how he could be so insightful one minute and so blind the next. How could he know the words she needed to hear concerning her mother, but be oblivious to the words she needed to hear concerning him? If only he would give her some sign or some hope that what he felt for her was more than a paternal affection.

"I understand," she lied, searching his face all the while for some sign of the love Ivy said he possessed. His eyes were warm when he looked at her, but he had already declared himself her protector. Maybe what she read in his expression was possessiveness. She suddenly wished her father was alive, if only so she could ask him about Brent. She had been a daddy's girl, and she knew that wouldn't have changed as she grew older. Her father had been loving, affectionate, and easy to talk to. He would have been her friend and guide.

Brent gave her shoulders a squeeze as he leaned down to bestow a kiss on her forehead. "We should go. I like to arrive first; it gives me an advantage."

"What sort of advantage?" she asked curiously as he came around to open her door and lift her down.

"Business," he said.

"But you're not really going to invest with him, are you?"

"Of course not," Brent replied. "But all of life is business, sug—there I go again." He reached up to scratch his head. "I had no idea I said 'sugar' so much until you pointed it out. I guess I got used to saying it with the horses. Anyway, the point is that, as a man, you have to approach everything in life as if it were a business deal. That's how you stay on top of the game."

She had never heard him talk this way, never seen the professional side of him, and it was a fascinating glimpse. The Honeywells were wealthy, but everyone assumed it was their father who kept them that way. Haley was beginning to think the brothers were shrewd businessmen in their own right, using their size and reputation to their advantage. If people thought they were stupid oafs, they wouldn't be as cautious in dealing with them, thereby giving the brothers a distinct edge because none of them was stupid. Oafish, maybe, but endearingly so, at least to Haley's way of thinking.

Brent clasped her hand, using it to lead her behind him as he approached the hostess and gave her his name. As if that were necessary. Haley knew by the look of terror in the woman's eye that Brent had been identified as a Honeywell the moment he stepped through the door. When the hostess looked around, assuring herself none of the other brothers were in tow, she relaxed and even managed a smile. Then she turned a speculative look on Haley. Most people in the community speculated about what sort of woman a Honeywell would settle down with, if one ever did.

He's not what you think, Haley wanted to protest. *He's gentle, and thoughtful, caring, and considerate. He's the best man you'll ever see.* Then again, Brent had cemented his reputation forever when he kidnapped the mayor's son a few years ago after witnessing him beating his horse with a whip. The mayor had blustered about bringing federal charges, but when his son arrived home after three days with the Honeywells, no talk of charges was ever mentioned again, and the family moved out of the area soon after the mayor lost his last election.

"What did you do to the mayor's son?" she blurted as soon as the hostess seated them and walked away.

Brent grinned at her. "I'll tell you sometime, but not right now. It's not polite dinner conversation."

The mention of dinner reminded Haley she was hungry. She picked up her menu and began to peruse the selections, but Brent seemed more intent on studying her. He picked up her hand and began gently toying with her fingers.

"I can't tell you how much I'm enjoying this time with you, Haley."

Haley set down her menu and leaned closer to him. "You could try," she said.

He laughed and lifted her hand to his mouth, skimming his lips over her knuckles. "You're a flirt, you bad kid."

"Does it bother you?" she asked.

"Not when you're flirting with me. I might have nightmares about you using your charms on some other man, though." He frowned and dropped his glance to his menu.

Emboldened by his display of jealousy, she pressed forward. "There's a simple remedy to that problem, Brent, and a sure way to make sure there are no other men."

He shifted uncomfortably, but before he could make a reply, Haley's mother and her boyfriend, Steve, arrived. Haley had only met Steve once, but he was exactly as she remembered: handsome, charming, and friendly. But, like the sickening sweetness of saccharine, Steve was as fake and left a similar bad taste on her tongue.

"Haley, sweetheart," Steve said gravely, taking her hand in his and clutching it tightly. "It's been much too long. Your mother and I have been worried sick about you."

As unobtrusively as she could, Haley snatched her hand out of his clasp and resisted the urge to wipe her palm on her skirt. She glanced at her mother to see if Steve's statement rang true, but her mother's expression was as remote as always. A pang of longing went through Haley at the sight of her mother, but she quickly suppressed it.

"Steve, Mother, how do you do?" She slid out of the booth and stood to give her mother their standard air kiss. Steve would have taken his turn embracing her, but Brent also stood and either his size or his proximity prohibited the action. Haley noted with some amusement that Steve had to look up several inches to see Brent's face, and she also realized he was unhappy about it.

"Let's sit down," he suggested eagerly, gesturing again toward the booth.

Brent stood aside, allowing Haley to slide to the center, and Steve did the same with her mother so the two women were sitting side by side. Steve wanted to jump right in and talk business, but Brent deftly subverted attention to Haley and her mother.

"Mrs. Griffin, I never realized before how much you and Haley look alike," he commented.

Mrs. Griffin gave her daughter an appraising stare. "Really, Mr. Honeywell, do you think so? I don't believe I've ever heard anyone make the comparison before." She picked up her menu and Haley did the same, frowning vaguely. Something told her that her mother hadn't been pleased by the comparison, but why? Was it because she didn't think Haley was as pretty as she was? Haley had always thought her mother was beautiful, but apparently the feeling wasn't mutual.

"Please call me Brent," Brent said, undeterred. "I'm surprised no one has pointed out the similarity between you two before. You could be sisters."

"I've always thought Haley looked more like her father," Mrs. Griffin said. She set down the menu with a pointed glare at Brent. Haley wondered why. Surely she didn't blame him for the accident, did she? And, even if she did, why would she care? She and Haley's father hadn't been happy. They had been teetering on the brink of divorce for months before the accident.

Haley rested her hand on Brent's knee, lest he take offense at her mother's unspoken accusations. "I think we look alike, Mama. Brent's not the only one who has said so."

"I heartily agree," Steve added. "Two pretty ladies, and aren't we lucky we know them both?" He shot Brent a conspiratorial leer over the table, which Brent didn't return.

Haley cleared her throat and turned to her mother. "What's new in your world, Mama? Have you redecorated the house to your satisfaction yet? The last time we spoke, you were trying to decide what color to paint the dining room."

"I painted the dining room almost two years ago. I've completely renovated the kitchen and the master suite since then."

"Oh," Haley said, trying not to let the lashing hurt take root. "I'm sure it looks lovely; you've always had good taste in decorating."

"It looks very nice," her mother agreed. Haley noted that she stopped short of inviting her to see for herself. An awkward silence settled over the table. Haley studied Brent as he ordered, trying to gauge his reaction to this meeting. He seemed to be holding himself back, trying to preserve judgment so he wouldn't say anything to make the situation worse.

When it was her turn to order, he rested his arm on the back of the booth, his hand lightly skimming her shoulders. She finished giving her order and he captured a tendril of hair, giving it a light tug. She looked at him, and he smiled and winked.

Out of her peripheral vision, she could almost see Steve rubbing his hands together in glee as he observed the exchange. If he thought his girlfriend's daughter had snagged a Honeywell, he would no doubt soon propose to her mother in order to make the tie official.

The waitress left, and Steve spoke. "Haley, honey, you've been keeping secrets. Last your mother and I knew, you and that other boy were together. We had no idea you'd moved on to Mr. Honeywell until I called his farm to check on you. You need to check in with us more often."

His chastising tone grated on her nerves. Why should she check in with him? He was nothing to her; she didn't even like him.

"Haley is being well taken care of," Brent assured him. "She's never been far from my care, and I'm up to date on all the facets of her life."

If the words were meant to be a warning, they were lost on Steve. "Yes, I know. I can't say I'm surprised you called this meeting, Brent. Her mother and I have been equally concerned about her."

Haley looked questioningly at Brent. What was Steve talking about? Apparently Brent didn't know, either.

"Why have you and Mrs. Griffin been concerned about Haley?" He leaned forward slightly and his grip tightened on Haley's shoulder.

"Because of the money, of course. Like you, we were hoping she would use it for college. But now that she hasn't, I think it's clear to see she's in over her head and needs some help figuring out what to do."

Haley wanted to crawl under the table. His blatant ruse in order to try and put himself in charge of her college fund was mortifying. That she should have any connection to this person was beyond embarrassing.

"The money isn't mine," Haley interjected. "It's Brent's, and I'm not touching it. He's going to take it back."

"The money is hers," Brent disagreed. "And I've set it up to stay that way."

"What does a twenty-year-old girl know about finances? Kids

today have no clue what it takes to handle such an investment," Steve said.

"Maybe some kids don't, but Haley isn't a kid. She's a grown woman with a good head on her shoulders, and I trust her to make the right decision where the money is concerned," Brent said. Steve started to speak again, but Brent held up his hand. "That's the end of the discussion, Mr. Owens. I hope we can have a civil conversation for the remainder of the meal; I'm finished talking business."

The waitress arrived with their drinks, momentarily averting any awkwardness Brent's announcement might cause. Haley's heart was thumping wildly. Did Brent mean what he said? Did he see her as a woman and not a child? Was Ivy correct? Did she have a chance with him?

The waitress left and Brent asked Steve a question about a new finance bill in Congress. Steve, to his credit, seemed to hold no ill will by having his attempts thwarted. He and Brent entered into a lively discussion while Haley turned toward her mother, trying vainly to think of a topic to discuss.

Her mother pulled out her phone and began scrolling through, either checking her call log or the internet.

"So, how are you, Mama?" Haley asked.

"Fine, Haley," she said, not taking her eyes off her phone.

"I've been well, too," Haley added, although her mother hadn't asked. "I'm still in the same apartment, although I'm looking for a new job." She glanced at Brent as thoughts of her job renewed her irritation with him. She thought he was deeply involved in his conversation with Steve, but he rested his hand on her knee and gave it a squeeze. She smiled, and he lightly squeezed her knee again.

"That's nice," her mother said absently.

Haley suppressed a sigh. Would the yearning for her mother's attention ever stop? At times like these she was always tempted to say something outrageous to see if her mother was paying attention. Would she put down her phone if Haley blurted she had been abducted by space aliens?

Her mother obviously wasn't in the mood for conversation, and

Haley had lost the heart to try. There was only so much rejection she could take, and her mother had given her a lifetime's worth already. Brent and Steve finished their conversation as their food arrived. Haley was thankful that Brent made the effort to make small talk while they ate. The rest of the evening remained shallow as they discussed the weather, local politics, and current events.

Finally, the meal was over. Haley breathed a sigh of relief as Steve and her mother stood to go. Steve shook her hand, as well as Brent's, and bid them a polite goodbye. Haley waited, hoping her mother would make the first move and hug her goodbye, but she didn't. In the end, she didn't even say goodbye. Brent shook her hand and she told him goodbye, turning away without a word to her daughter.

Haley watched her walk away, swallowing down the pain that was always present when she was near her mother. Brent's arm stole around her shoulders.

"Come on, sweetheart. Let's go home."

Home. The word was a bitter pill for Haley. She had an apartment, but it wasn't her home. She had no home, and she hadn't since her father died. He had been her home and when he went, he took all love, comfort, and security with him.

She had given up pitying herself long ago, or at least she thought she had. Right now, she wanted nothing more than to wallow in misery and feel sorry for herself.

"When is the last time you saw you mother?" Brent asked when they were safely tucked in his truck.

"Almost two years ago." There was a time that Haley called her mother at regular intervals, stopped by, and arranged get-togethers. Then at their last meeting it was as if a lightbulb went off. Haley realized that, not only was she the one doing all the talking, but she was also always the one who made arrangements. She decided to wait for her mother to reach out to her. She was still waiting.

"What did you do for Christmas last year?" Brent asked.

"On Christmas Eve, I got together with a few of my friends for breakfast."

"What about Christmas day?"

She looked out her window, remembering the sadness and loneliness of that day. Thoughts of him were the only thing that had gotten her through. She had propped his card on her table and looked at it all day long, saving it until before she went to bed that night so she would have something to look forward to in the long, dreary day.

"Did you have a tree?" Brent asked softly.

"Trees are expensive." She tried to say it casually, as if spending Christmas alone hadn't bothered her. And, really, it hadn't been so bad. The actual day was sad, but the next day the feelings faded and life returned to normal.

"Did you have presents?"

She sighed. Why was he prolonging this line of questioning? "From you," she said.

He didn't respond. When she turned to look at him, his lips were pressed in a tight line, and he was gripping the steering wheel. Was he angry at her mother for her abandonment? Or was he angry at Haley for not reaching out and informing him of her dreary situation? With Brent, it was hard to tell.

They arrived at the farm, and he lifted her down from the truck without a word. When they reached the front door, he turned to her with a smile that seemed forced.

"I think I'll spend some time with my baby sister before she has to head back to Montana. You make yourself at home."

They strode into the living room together. He glanced at Ivy, picked her up, threw her over his shoulder, and left the room.

Coy was holding baby Jess. He listened to his wife's squeals of protest with a frown. "You'd think I would get used to that, but I never do."

"Take heart," Haley said. "Someday he's going to be too old to lift her over his head."

Coy laughed. "With Number One, I don't think that day will ever get here. He's perpetually fifteen, as far as I'm concerned. Maybe you can help him grow up a little."

Haley smiled, but she had no energy for banter today. Jess was awake and cooing, so Haley leaned over and began to talk to her. Coy handed her off, and they spent the next couple of hours playing together on the floor until it was the baby's bedtime. There was still no sign of Brent. She wandered to the den where Grant was watching a movie. It was an action movie, and his gaze was intently fastened on the screen, but he moved aside and made room for her on the sofa when she entered the room.

"Are you going to marry Brent?" he said a few minutes later. Since he still hadn't taken his gaze from the television, it took her a few seconds to process the question.

"I suppose that's up to him," she said.

He nodded and remained staring unblinkingly at the TV. She tried to concentrate on the television, too, but the movie was already half over. Instead, she rested her head on the end of the sofa and began to doze. The movie must have ended because Grant turned off the television.

"Are you sleeping out here?" he asked, startling her awake. "I would carry you to your bed, but I don't think Brent would like that, and I don't want to wind up with a broken jaw like Corliss."

"I'll walk," she said. She stumbled down the hall toward her room, still feeling half asleep, but when she went to bed she lay there a long time. Where was Brent? Why had he disappeared? Was he angry with her? She had a sudden longing for the simplicity of Tyler. Even when they were teenagers, she had never lain in bed trying to figure him out. With that thought, she finally fell asleep.

CHAPTER 14

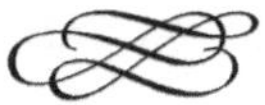

*H*azy light woke Haley early the next morning. She squinted toward the window, but the light streaming behind the slits in the curtain looked clear and bright. That meant the soft light must be coming from inside the room, but she didn't usually sleep with a nightlight. Had she inadvertently left the bathroom light on when she went to bed last night?

She sat up to look. "Oh," she said, startled by the sight of a Christmas tree twinkling in the corner.

"Oh, good, you're awake."

She yelped as Brent rolled over on the floor and looked up at her. He was wearing his clothes, but he had clearly just woken up. "Did you sleep in here?" she asked.

He checked his watch. "Only for the last hour or so." He smiled. "Merry Christmas."

"It's October," she pointed out.

"But you missed Christmas last year. We're having a redo."

She looked at the tree again. From the smell of fresh pine, she knew it was a real tree. It was fully decorated and lit. "There are presents," she exclaimed.

"This is your morning for stating the obvious," Brent said cheerfully. He sat up and drew his knees to his chest. "Of course there are presents. It's Christmas."

"I didn't get you any presents," she said.

"You didn't know it was going to be Christmas," he said patiently. "Are you getting out of bed now?"

She smiled at the enthusiastic look on his face, remembering Coy's comment about Brent being forever fifteen. Right now he looked even younger, and more eager than anyone she had ever seen. "I'm not dressed."

"I don't mind seeing your pajamas," he said.

She dropped the sheet she was holding to her chest, revealing her pretty ivory lingerie.

Brent darted to his feet and practically sprinted for the door. "I'll, uh, wait in the hallway while you change."

Haley chuckled when he slammed the door in his haste to reach the safety of the corridor. She wanted to shower, blow dry her hair, and apply makeup, but she knew that would take a long time and Brent was probably already losing patience. Instead she settled for getting dressed, running a brush through her hair, brushing her teeth, and applying some lip gloss before opening the door to let him back in.

He took her hand and led her close to the tree, then placed his hands on her shoulders and gave her a light push so she would sit down. He sat cross-legged beside her and handed her a present from the stack. She looked at it and at him. "How did you do this?"

"Ivy helped me. She's really good at this sort of thing, the decorating and picking out presents, I mean. I hope it's okay that she helped. I had final approval on her selections, but I couldn't get everything done by myself."

She set the present aside and closed the distance between them, hugging him tightly around the neck. "I think it's more than okay, I think it's wonderful. This is the sweetest thing anyone has ever done for me."

"You haven't opened the presents yet," he said. He pressed his palms to her back and held her close. "You might change your mind if they're bad and you don't like them."

"I don't need presents. The thoughtfulness of the tree is enough. Thank you."

He let her go and reached for a present. "If you don't need these, maybe I should take them all away."

She swatted his hand. "Don't touch my presents."

He sat back with a smile and waited for her to begin the opening process. She tore open a rectangular box and let out a squeal of delight when a cashmere sweater fell out. "This is so beautiful." She rubbed the soft material over her cheek and closed her eyes. When she opened her eyes, Brent was watching her with a warm smile.

"Open this one next," he commanded, shoving another box in her hands. "They go together."

The next box revealed a pair of tailored pants that would look perfect with the sweater. She had never owned something so grown up or professional-looking before, and she smiled in delight. Ivy certainly had good taste in clothes.

"Here, maybe you can use these for the remainder of your visit," Brent said uncomfortably as he handed her the next box. She laughed when she pulled out a pair of satin pajamas.

"You don't approve of my sleeping attire?" she asked with mock innocence.

"I...they're, uh..." He paused and tugged at the collar of his shirt. "Next present." He stuffed another box in her hands and studiously ignored her laughter.

The next box was a book, one that Haley had been intending to read for the last few months. After that was a gift card and then some cashmere socks to match the sweater. "This is too much," Haley said as she looked at the purchases strewn around her feet. "I love them, all of them, but I'm overwhelmed."

"There's one more," Brent said. "I picked this one all by myself." He pulled a small velvet box from his pocket and held it in the palm of his hand.

Halcy blinked at it, dazed. Surely he wasn't going to propose, was he? For a split second, she felt a small measure of panic. Then she realized that if the box contained an engagement ring, there would be no hesitation on her part. She loved this man, and she wanted to spend the rest of her life with him. He pushed the box closer. Haley's heart thumped heavily as he used his other hand to open it.

"Earrings," she said. She hadn't meant to reveal her disappointment in her tone, but somehow she must have because Brent's smile slipped into a frown.

"To match the necklace." He reached forward and touched the necklace he had given her for her sixteenth Christmas. "But if you'd rather exchange it for something you choose yourself, that's okay." He started to close the box and withdraw it, but Haley held out her hand.

"No, I love them. They're beautiful, and they match perfectly. Really," she added when he looked uncertain. She took the box from him and gave the earrings a closer inspection. They really were lovely; they were diamonds, and they were huge.

"Are you sure? I know sometimes women like to choose their own jewelry." She hated that her less-than-stellar reaction was causing him to doubt whether or not she liked his present. She set aside the box and eased closer to him, once again hugging him tightly around the neck.

"Brent, I love them. I think they're beautiful. This has been the best morning of my life, and I'll never forget it. Thank you." She pressed a kiss to his cheek and lingered. She had simply meant to bestow a friendly kiss of gratitude, but his tangy cologne wafted toward her, giving her pause. Brent's arms eased comfortably around her, but the longer she remained pressed to his face, the tighter his grip became on the back of her shirt.

She lightly rubbed her nose over his stubbly cheek. He squeezed his eyes shut and swallowed hard.

"Um, Haley," he said.

"Hmm," she replied absently as she continued her tactile inspection of his face. Without thinking, she leaned closer, nibbling slightly on his earlobe before she found herself unceremoniously dumped on the floor. Brent stood towering over her, looking flustered.

"Breakfast is probably ready. We should go. I'll meet you there so you can get these things sorted and put away." He turned and dashed out of the room.

Haley lay sprawled on the floor, trying to figure out what happened. *Good thing I'm flexible,* she thought as she took in her legs, which were now bent at an impossible angle. She wasn't sure Brent could have gotten away any faster, and she felt the sting of his rejection all the way to her toes. "Ouch," she said, both because of his rebuff and because her legs were starting to cramp. She unfolded herself from her pretzel-like configuration and then did as he suggested, sorting her presents and packing them in her suitcase. The action provided her with an outlet so she didn't have to think of what had passed between her and Brent. Could he possibly make it any clearer that he wasn't interested in her?

Yes, she thought. *He could stop confusing me by treating me like he's in love with me one minute and fleeing from me in terror the next.*

When she emerged from her bedroom, she realized the name of the game was going to be denial. Brent looked up with a greeting smile that belied any awkwardness that may have existed between them.

"Morning," he said cheerfully, scooting his chair aside so she could ease in beside him.

"Good morning," she said slowly, trying to find her footing.

Coy and Ivy arrived, baby Jess in tow. "Good morning," Brent boomed. Coy gave him a suspicious look before quirking an eyebrow at Haley. She shrugged one shoulder. "What are you two up to today?" Brent continued.

"We were going to visit some of my roommates from college, but Mom has a church meeting today and can't watch Jess. I guess we'll hang around here today and do the roommate thing tomorrow," Ivy said.

"We'll watch Jess for you," Brent said.

"You don't have to do that. We can wait until tomorrow," Ivy said.

"No, we'll do it. We'd love to," Brent declared.

"Wow, Haley, I didn't even see your lips move when you volunteered to babysit for us," Coy said.

"Haley loves kids," Brent said. He sounded a little desperate.

"I do love kids," Haley agreed. "And I would love to watch Jess today." And she was irritated with Brent who was clearly ready to do anything in order not to be alone with her, even if it meant spending the entire day with an infant.

"Okay," Ivy drawled. "Then I guess we're going out today. Excuse me while I call my friends to make arrangements." She took out her phone and pushed away from the table.

"Don't let him take Jess on a horse," Coy said to Haley. Haley laughed until Brent interjected.

"Is Ivy still telling that story? Look, I was only seven. How was I to know newborns weren't supposed to ride horses? And, besides, I didn't drop her. Everything turned out fine."

"And don't let him feed her anything," Coy added.

"I didn't know babies couldn't chew things," Brent said. "Ivy was fine as soon as Mom Heimliched her."

"And don't let him teach her to play with fire," Coy went on.

"I didn't think she would actually touch the flame," Brent said. "The burns were only first degree. She didn't even scar."

"And don't let him…" Coy began again, but Brent interrupted.

"I'm not going to hurt Jess. Ivy was my learning curve. We'll be fine."

"I know you will," Coy said confidently. "As long as Haley's in charge. Listen to her and do what she says."

Brent grimaced at his patronizing tone, but didn't retaliate. "Don't you have somewhere to be?" he asked instead.

Coy grinned and picked up his Stetson from a nearby chair. "I suppose I'll go and take advantage of this rare alone time with my wife. Haley, you have our number if he does anything you don't approve of with Jess. Or with you."

Haley laughed as Coy ducked out of the room, leaving a blustering Brent in his wake. "What did he mean by that?" he demanded. "What would I do with you that you wouldn't approve of?"

"Absolutely nothing," Haley said dryly. Brent frowned, but Haley ignored him and picked up Jess who had started to fuss when her parents left the room. She tapped a few pieces of dissolvable cereal in front of them and smiled as she watched Jess pick up a piece and try to direct her fat fist to her mouth. The fist waved frantically as it tried to find its mark.

After breakfast, they took Jess for a walk around the farm, passing her off when she became cumbersome. Mostly it was Haley who had to do the passing. Jess was tiny, but even a few pounds became heavy after a while, at least for her. Brent could probably have carried her all day, but she seemed to prefer Haley and kept reaching for her.

When they arrived home, it was time for Jess's nap. Haley changed her and put her down, easing out of the room as Jess's eyes became heavier and heavier. Brent was waiting for her in the hallway and together they walked to the family room. Since the rest of the family was working, they were alone in the large house, except for Sandy who was in the kitchen. They sat on the couch and Brent clasped her hand.

"You're good with kids," he declared. "Maybe you should get your degree in education."

"Maybe," she agreed. "Although I'd rather have a whole bunch of my own."

He blinked a few times, assimilating that information. "How many do you want?"

"Four seems like a good place to start."

"I'm from a large family."

"Yes, I know," she said. "I've met you before, remember?"

"People don't seem to want large families these days," he continued, undaunted by her sarcasm.

"Well I do." Psychologists could probably have a field day with her reason why, but Haley didn't care. She wanted to have a lot of kids so she could give them all the love and attention she had missed out on as a child.

"I do, too," Brent said.

But not with me, Haley thought. She wanted to shake the sense into him, to tell him they were perfect for each other and she was right in front of him, ripe for the plucking. Short of that, there was only one other thing she could do: she could take herself out of the running. "I need to go home tomorrow," she said.

He flinched as if she'd hit him. "Why?"

"Because you said a week and it's been a week."

"It's been five days," he said.

"Close enough."

"Stay through the weekend," he pled.

She shook her head. Now that she had made the decision, she knew it was the right one. "I've already taken you away from Ivy and Coy too much. You need to spend this time with your family, and I need to go home and start looking for a job."

"Use the money and go to college," he said, exasperated.

"No. No way. The money isn't mine, it's yours. I'll find a job and pay my own way to college."

He dropped her hand and let out a breath, running his fingers through his hair. "Haley, if this is about what happened this morning…"

"What did happen this morning?" she asked.

"Nothing," he said earnestly. "Nothing happened. We were hugging. Things started to get a little carried away, that's all. But nothing happened, nothing either of us will regret."

"You mean nothing you will regret," she said.

"I mean both of us. You don't know what you're getting into here. You're a…"

She pressed her fingers to his lips. "If you say I'm a kid, I'm leaving right now and walking home."

He smiled against her fingertips. "You're a sweetheart," he said, though she was sure that wasn't what he had originally intended to say. "If you're bound and determined to leave tomorrow, then let's have a pleasant remainder of the day with no arguing, okay?"

"Sounds wonderful," she said. "Want to watch a movie until Jess wakes up?"

"Maybe you could read to me if you don't mind," he said. "I've actually heard good things about that book you got for Christmas this morning."

"Okay," she said. She couldn't have been more surprised if he had suggested hula dancing. She hadn't taken Brent for a reader. She sprinted to her room to retrieve the book. They sat on opposite ends of the couch with their feet up and facing each other. She started to read and he picked up her foot, massaging the ball until her bones and muscles felt like jelly. When the massage came to an abrupt end, she looked up to see him fast asleep, his head tilted toward the couch.

"Brent," she whispered, but he didn't stir. "I love you," she added. Then she set aside the book and took her own nap until they heard Jess begin to stir on the monitor.

They spent the next few hours playing with Jess, and then the rest of the family began to filter in. Coy and Ivy returned and reclaimed their daughter before everyone sat down to a family dinner. For Haley, who was an only child and estranged from her only living parent, the scene was like something from a fairy tale. Even the feud between Coy and the brothers seemed idyllic in light of her lonely existence. Melancholy began to steal over her at the thought that this was her last night here. What would happen to her and Brent after she went away? Would they go back to the way it was with him over-seeing her wellbeing from a safe distance? Would they see each other occasionally so that he could convince himself he was her benevolent benefactor and nothing more?

When he rested his arm on the back of her chair and began absently playing with her hair, she wondered if he was thinking the same thing. What went on in his head was anyone's guess. To Haley's way of thinking, they'd had a perfect week, one that proved the age difference between them didn't matter. They cared about each other, they were compatible, they were attracted to each other. What more was there? Why should the year they were born have anything to do with it?

After supper, they had the family room to themselves again. Even though the house was large, the fact that none of the ten people present were using this room was a little fishy to Haley. Was the family purposely giving them time alone together? That didn't seem like the sort of thing the brothers would do, but maybe Ivy had told them to. Whatever the reason, Haley was happy for the privacy, and Brent appeared to be, too. He stretched out on the sofa and pulled her down beside him, slinging one arm over her waist. With his free hand, he stretched toward the end table and retrieved her book.

"You'll have to go back a couple of chapters because I don't remember much from this afternoon," he said.

She backtracked to the place where she thought he had stopped listening and began reading. A few minutes later, the sound of his even, steady breathing alerted her to the fact that he was once again asleep. She stopped reading aloud, but continued reading silently to herself while Brent slept. If she had to pin a label on what she was feeling, it would be contentment. Lying beside Brent and reading quietly was better than anything she had ever done with anyone else. She knew without a doubt she could spend every day for the rest of her life the same way and never grow bored. Brent's affection was all-consuming without being smothering. Tyler had always treated her well, but it wasn't the same thing. Brent *cherished* her, and that made all the difference. Except for urging her to go to college, he didn't try to change her. He accepted her completely but, even more than that, he adored her. She could feel the discrepancy and she knew if Brent rejected her she would probably never find anyone who treated her the same way.

About an hour later she felt his eyes on her and knew he was awake. She set aside her book and looked down to see him smiling sleepily at her. He cinched his arm closer, pulling her farther down beside him.

"See what happens when you get old? You can't even stay awake through one chapter," he whispered.

"Maybe you fell asleep because you stayed up all night making Christmas for me," she said.

"Nah, I'm old," he said. His finger traced lightly over her lashes. "Too old for…everything."

"Brent, you can't really believe that. You're thirty two. That's not old. You have years and years and years left. The question is what are you going to do with them?"

He smiled faintly. "We promised not to discuss unpleasant topics tonight."

"Why is your future an unpleasant topic?"

He remained mute, gently trailing his fingertip over her face. She closed her eyes, giving in to his relaxing ministrations. "Maybe *I'm* old because you're making me sleepy, and I already took a nap today." They were quiet a few minutes and she felt herself slipping toward unconsciousness when he spoke again.

"Don't go home tomorrow," he whispered. "Please stay a little longer."

She opened her eyes and pressed her palm to his cheek. "Give me a reason."

Conflict raged in his expression, and she wondered why. Was it because he didn't care for her the way she wanted him to, or was it something else? The longer he went without giving her an answer, the more sure she was of her decision.

"I think it's best if I go tomorrow," she said, trying hard to keep her voice neutral. He hadn't promised her anything, and therefore she had no right to be upset with him. He had already given her so much; what right did she have to expect more? She was

disappointed in his lack of response, but she would keep it to herself.

"I'm going to miss you," he said. "You've been part of my world for fifteen years, but in a peripheral way. This week everything seemed real. You're a part of me."

She didn't get her hopes up that he was sending her a coded message about his secret love. If he loved her, he would say so. Instead, she smiled and clasped his hand, giving it a squeeze. "And you're a part of me." *The biggest part; the best part.*

"Are we going to see each other after you go home?" he asked.

"I guess that's up to you."

"Why is it up to me?"

"Because you're the busy professional. My schedule is pretty open now that I'm unemployed."

"I'll help you find a job if that's what you want. We'll start looking tomorrow."

"Sounds good," she said. Anything that prolonged her time with him sounded good. They looked at each other a while longer. She traced the bump in his nose, wondering how he broke it and guessing it had something to do with his brothers. "I should probably go to bed. I really am getting sleepy."

"Stay," he said, tightening his grip on her waist. "We can read awhile longer."

"I can't read," she said. "My eyes are blurring."

"I'll read to you." He reached over her, inadvertently smashing her into the couch, and picked up the book. He started on the open page, his voice a gentle whisper near her ear. She smiled, closed her eyes, and the next thing she knew it was morning and she was waking up fully clothed in her bed.

CHAPTER 15

*H*aley and Brent were somber the next morning at breakfast. As if sensing their mood, everyone else was quiet, too, even baby Jess. Brent sat on her bed and sullenly watched her as she packed. At one point she stopped and tapped his protruding lip.

"You're pouting," she said.

"You're leaving," he replied. "I'm allowed."

She snapped her case closed and handed it to him. He carried it to his truck and tossed it in the back seat before picking up Haley and tossing her inside, too. She had already said her farewells and thanks to his family. Her cheek still tingled with warmth from his mother's kiss. Haley hadn't been expecting that, and she would have teared up, if not for the amusing sight of baby Jess once again trying to bring her chubby fist to her mouth. She had already kissed the baby, but she went over to do it again. That was when Coy had leaned in to whisper, "I'm pulling for you." When she almost teared up over that, Haley realized she was simply emotional this morning and needed to go, the sooner the better.

Now she and Brent were finally on the road, and she felt like she had a better handle on her wayward feelings. She wasn't sure Brent did, though. He sat forward, gripping the steering wheel and swallowing hard. When she realized how often she had observed him driving in that same, tense pose, she looked around at where they were with dawning understanding.

"Stop," she said, startling him so he tore his eyes from the road and looked at her in concern. "Pull over," she commanded.

He did so, putting the truck into park and turning it off. "What's wrong? Did you forget something? Do we need to turn around?"

"No, it's nothing like that. I realized you tense up every time we drive through the intersection."

"What intersection?" he asked with unconvincing ignorance.

"Brent," she pressed, "you're anxious every time you pass by this spot, aren't you?"

He looked around uncomfortably, realizing for the first time that he had stopped in the exact spot where he had first pulled Haley from her car. "I'm fine," he said, but she didn't believe him.

"You're not fine. Is it a post trauma reaction, or is it something else?" When he remained silent, she took off her seatbelt and slid closer, resting her hand lightly on his forearm. "What is it? Please tell me."

He shook his head.

"I was part of that day, too," she said.

"As if I could forget that," he choked.

The sudden silence between them was oppressive. "What's that supposed to mean?"

He finally looked at her, and when he did, she flinched. "I killed your father, Haley. I took the one person who loved you out of your life. How could I ever forget that or let it go? Every time I drive through here, I remember. It's like my own personal torture device."

"Brent, you can't tell me you blame yourself for the accident. Everyone agreed it wasn't your fault."

"But no one else was here. I should have been paying closer attention. I should have noticed him sooner. I should have slowed down when I neared the intersection. I should have done *something*."

"There was nothing you could have done."

He shook his head, and she tightened her grip on his hand. "Listen to me because I'm going to tell you something I've never told anyone else before, something I've kept hidden all these years." She paused, gathering her courage. "I think my father drove through the intersection on purpose that day. I think he was trying to kill himself and me, too."

"Don't say that," Brent choked.

"It's true," Haley said. "I've had a lot of time to think about it. He and my mother had been having problems. They had already told me they were getting divorced. His behavior before the accident was odd. He and my mother had a horrible argument. He picked me up, loaded me in the car, and drove. He was driving crazy, and even I knew it. I told him to put on his seatbelt, and he didn't listen. It was like he was in another world. I saw you coming. I screamed at him to stop, and I swear he accelerated." She squeezed his arm again. "I've never blamed you, Brent. How could I? You're the best thing that's ever happened to me."

"Don't say that," Brent said. "I've only tried to do what's right by you." He ground his palms into his eye sockets and took a few shuddering breaths as he tried to collect himself. Meanwhile Haley felt like she was falling apart.

"That's what this has all been about? All these years you've been trying to find atonement?"

"There is no atonement for taking a man's life," he said.

She eased away from him, sliding back toward her seat. "I'm ready to go home now."

The quiet dignity in her voice finally broke through his emotional turmoil and he looked at her, noting her gray pallor. "What's wrong with you?"

She shook her head. Now it was his turn to remove his seatbelt and slide across the seat. "Haley, tell me," he commanded.

"All this time, I thought you watched over me because I was special to you, because you…But it's all been about trying to make amends for something you didn't even do. I'm nothing to you."

He placed his hands on her shoulders and gave her a shake. "How could you say that? You know what passed between us that day, the bond that was forged. I stayed in your life because I wanted to, because I care about you."

She was beyond being able to hear him—the pain went too deep. All she heard was that, like her mother, he had only been a part of her life because of obligation. She didn't know she was crying until he pointed it out.

"Ah, Haley, don't cry. Please, please don't cry, baby." He let go her shoulders to cup her face, kissing her cheeks fervently. Either instinct or desperation caused her to turn her head slightly so that one of his kisses missed her cheek and hit her mouth, and that small act was the catalyst they needed to break through the tension that had been simmering between them all week.

For years, Haley had dreamed about what it would be like to kiss Brent, but the reality was better than any fantasy. He kissed the same way he did everything else, with total devotion. All sense of time, space, self, and even reality were stripped away as the kiss went on and on and on. Finally, he pulled himself away and skidded to his side of the car gripping the steering wheel for support as he tried to get a breath.

Haley felt euphoric at having her suspicions confirmed. She hadn't imagined what had been happening between them all week; Brent had felt it, too, and at last he had acted on it. Only he hadn't meant to, a fact which soon became all too apparent.

"I'm sorry," he said sincerely after a solid two minutes of silence.

"Sorry," she repeated the word as if she had never heard it, mostly because she couldn't figure its meaning in reference to the amazing kiss they had shared. "Why are you sorry?"

"Because that shouldn't have happened. I shouldn't have lost control like that."

"Yes you should have, and you should do it a lot more," Haley said.

He banged his fist on the steering wheel. "Haley, this is serious. I can't go around kissing you like that when I'm supposed to be your guardian."

"You are not my guardian," she said vehemently.

"You know what I mean. The relationship we have is more like a mentorship than a romance."

For the second time in the space of a half hour, her jaw dropped in astonishment. "A mentorship? Do you always cuddle on couches with your mentees? Do you buy them beautiful and expensive earrings?"

"I'll admit the lines have been a little blurred this week, but that's what I've been trying to tell you. We're friends, but that's all we can ever be." Apparently he found something outside the window fascinating because it was all he would look at.

"Why?" she whispered. She didn't trust her voice enough to use it out loud.

"You know why," he said. "I'm too old for you. You're too young for me. And, besides that, I've known you since you were five. And whether you believe it or not, I'm at least partially responsible for your father's death. There's too much baggage between us, and too many years. You and I will never be more than what we are now." He finally dragged his gaze to hers. "But I think what we are now is pretty great, don't you?"

She must have nodded because he gave her a slight smile. "See? We'll forget this little interlude ever happened and go back to the way things were."

Did she nod again? She didn't know, but apparently she must have done something to give assent because he started the truck again. They made the rest of the drive to her apartment in silence. He reached for the ignition when he pulled into her parking lot, but she stopped him.

"Don't," she croaked. "Don't come in. I need some time and some space. I have to think things through."

His hand remained on the ignition and she knew he was deciding if he was going to grant her request or bulldoze his way into her apartment to hash things out. "All right," he agreed at last. "If that's what you want."

"It is," she said.

She stood back while he carried her bags to the lobby. She picked them up and carried them the remaining length to her apartment, not turning to give him another glance, even though she knew he was watching her walk away.

CHAPTER 16

Two weeks. Brent had given Haley two weeks to cool off, but enough was enough. If she hadn't called by this evening, he was going to track her down and make her talk to him. He didn't like to think about the fact that he had technically only given her one week to cool off; for the past week, she hadn't been returning his calls.

He frowned, staring vacantly at the stack of papers in his hand. Why hadn't she returned his calls? And why was she so angry in the first place? Surely she could understand that he was doing what was best for her, that he always did what was best for her. Though, in retrospect, she hadn't seemed angry that last day in the car. She had seemed hurt. But that wasn't possible, was it? How could she be hurt when he hadn't intended to hurt her? Maybe she had a misplaced crush on him, and maybe things had gotten a little intense between them, but she didn't really think they had a future, did she? How could she when she was a young and beautiful girl and he was...well, maybe he wasn't old. But he was getting there.

His mind wandered and he let it, thinking about the week they had spent together. It had been perfect, which only made her absence more profound. He tried to remember the last time he had felt so hollow but couldn't. He had never felt as empty as he felt now without Haley. Tonight he was going to make her talk to him. He would clear up the confusion between them so they could get back on track to wherever it was they were going. His frown deepened to a scowl. No, that wasn't right. They weren't going anywhere except friendship. He would clear things up so they could get their friendship back on track.

But when Corliss stuck his head in the office, thoughts of Haley temporarily fled his mind.

"We still on for tonight?" Corliss asked. Over the last few weeks, Brent had become adept at interpreting the murmurs his brother made without moving his lips.

"Yes. Is everyone coming?"

Corliss nodded. He would have smiled, but he couldn't. "I've never looked forward to anything more than I am to getting these things off." He tapped his cheek and ducked back out of the office.

Brent's smile lasted until he disappeared, then he picked up the phone and dialed Haley again. "It's me. Again. I don't know why you won't call me back, but this avoidance doesn't seem like you, and I don't like it. I'm giving you until tomorrow, and then I'm going to track you down, and then we're going to..." His mind flashed to the kiss they had shared in his truck. "And then we're going to talk," he finished lamely. He closed his phone and took a breath, squinching his eyes tightly closed.

There was an endless stack of work on his desk—exponentially higher since he took the week off to be with Haley—but he couldn't make himself concentrate on legal jargon today.

"Focus," he told himself, then he buckled down and did exactly that, working diligently until Corliss came to retrieve him at the end of the day.

All five brothers filed out of the office together, single file, and piled in Brent's truck. They drove Corliss to his doctor in Lexington, and filled up the waiting room with their presence while they waited.

Corliss emerged, wire free and smiling as he gently massaged his jaw. "Let's get some steak," he said cheerfully. "That's one thing that a blender definitely doesn't do justice to. I'm in the mind to chew."

"Think we could try Ruby's again?" Everett asked. Ruby's was a steakhouse that was more pub than restaurant. The brothers had been thrown out and told not to return, but that was a year ago. They found that most places were willing to give them another try after about a year.

"Ruby's has the best steak around," Grant declared. "It's worth a shot."

"Ruby's it is," Brent decreed.

They entered cautiously, as unobtrusively as possible. The hostess worriedly bit her lip when she caught sight of them, but she didn't call for help or scowl, both good signs. She even managed a smile when she delivered their menus, then smiled and blushed faintly when Darcy winked at her.

"We'll have five of the special," Corliss said. They had agreed ahead of time that they would order from the menu in order to ensure as little fuss as possible.

"I'll let your waitress know," the hostess said politely as she made her exit.

The brothers let out a collective sigh of relief. They had done it; they were going to be allowed to eat at Ruby's again. Even Brent, who was still feeling dejected, was cheered again at being allowed entrée into one of their favorite restaurants.

The meal arrived without incident. At first the waitress's hand shook as she poured their tea, but by the end of the meal she was laughing and bantering with them.

"I think we're really getting the hang of this restaurant thing," Everett said.

"Maybe word will spread and we'll be allowed to some of the others," Grant said, his tone hopeful.

A man approached them, someone none of them had ever seen before. He looked at Corliss with a glare of hatred. "Aren't you the Honeywell who used to go with Allie?"

Corliss tensed, his hand tightening on his fork. "Who wants to know?"

"Her cousin, that's who. I know what you did to her. I know why she went away, and if you think I'm going to keep it a secret, then you're crazy."

Corliss set down his fork and dabbed his lips with his napkin before speaking. "Mister, you'd better walk away right now."

"Are you going to make me, you miserable piece of filth? I brought a couple of buddies with me. Maybe it's you who needs to step outside, or are you afraid to go without your brothers for protection."

"Walk away," Corliss said as the man's three friends stepped up and glowered.

"Do they know?" the man asked. He gestured toward the other Honeywells. "Do they know what you did to Allie? Do they know how you..."

He stopped speaking abruptly when Corliss's fist connected with his face. After a second of stunned surprise, his friends joined in the fray, jumping on Corliss and attempting to take him to the ground.

"Here we go," Everett said, tossing his napkin to the table.

"So much for Ruby's," Darcy agreed, then the other brothers jumped onto the pile of bodies on the floor and started punching.

Three hours later when they emerged from the hospital, Corliss's jaw was wired shut again. "They should have told me it was still broken. I thought when they took the wires off it meant I was completely healed," he murmured.

"If you knew it was still fragile, would it have kept you from punching that guy?" Darcy asked.

"No, but I would have guarded my face better." He gave a rueful shake of his head. "I'm getting old. I used to be able to take a punch better than this."

"We're all getting old," Brent added darkly. He pulled out his phone and checked his messages, but there were none. A glance at his watch told him it was too late to see Haley tonight. He would have to try again in the morning.

"Why didn't we get arrested this time?" Everett asked.

"We didn't damage anything in the restaurant this time, and with Corliss's broken jaw, I think they thought we were the victims for once," Brent explained.

"They didn't break my jaw," Corliss mumbled. "You make sure and tell them you're the one who broke my jaw, and not some stranger," he told Brent.

"I'll see what I can do," Brent said, although he didn't mean it. As the family's legal advisor, he sometimes had to do what he thought best, even if it meant overriding his brothers' pride. Although it rankled him to think outsiders might believe someone else had broken Corliss's jaw. No one had ever taken down a Honeywell before, and not for lack of trying. Tonight had been no exception. Grant had sat out the fight so it would be an even four on four, and still they had quickly subdued their opponents, almost to the point where the other four men were crying and begging for mercy.

"Four more weeks," Corliss burbled. "Four more weeks of a liquid diet, a diet I have to make for myself because Sandy won't do it for me."

"Can't you talk to her and explain what happened with Allie?" Everett asked.

"How can I explain it when I don't understand it myself?" Corliss said. "Maybe I should go away for a while."

"Where would you go?" Grant asked.

Corliss shrugged. "I don't know. Maybe to visit our baby sister for a while."

The brothers looked aghast. "You would turn tale and run to Montana? Like a coward?" Darcy said.

"It would be nice to get away from the situation and maybe stop thinking about Allie all the time," Corliss said.

The three younger brothers piled in the back of the truck while Brent drove and Corliss sat in the front.

"You really still think about Allie all the time?" Brent asked, softly so the other brothers wouldn't hear.

Corliss nodded and winced when the motion upset his jaw.

"Do you love her?" Brent pressed.

"I miss her. I think about her always, and when I do, it hurts because she's gone. If that's love, then, yes, I guess I love her."

Brent sat forward, gripping the steering wheel. His brother's words echoed in his head. *If that's love, then, yes, I guess I love her.* The way Corliss had described his feelings for Allie was exactly the way Brent felt about Haley. But he wasn't in love with her, was he? She was a kid.

They arrived home, and he sought the solace of his room. Reaching up to the top of his closet, he pulled down a box and began to sift through it. There were notes from Haley, one for every year since they met. He smiled as he picked up the oldest one and saw her girlish handwriting, barely discernable, thanking him for her birthday flowers. As the years progressed, so did her handwriting skills and the length of the letters. Starting in middle school, she had penned missives that lasted for a couple of pages, letting him in on all the happenings of her little girl world. He had loved receiving the letters each year; they had almost been like talking to her, though sometimes they made him sad. She probably hadn't meant to be so transparent, but he had seen through her happy chatter to the lonely little girl whose father was gone and whose mother wanted no part of her life.

His smile died when he came to the last two letters, the two he had received since she turned eighteen. These were different than the rest; they were formal, simply telling him thanks and wishing him well. Why had she stopped spilling her secrets to him? Why did she stop wearing her heart on her sleeve?

Because she grew up, he told himself. *She became a woman and stopped revealing the inner workings of her heart to a stranger.* The word pained him. Was he a stranger to Haley? Had she thought of him that way? Was that why she had stopped pouring out her heart? Or was there another reason? He sat up, gripping the letters so tightly he was in danger of crushing them.

Maybe Haley didn't want him to know what was in her heart because it was about him. Maybe what he had been playing down as a teenage crush was actually something much more. Could it be that she was actually in love with him? And was it possible that he was in love with her?

An hour later, he was still staring at his closet, and he still didn't have the answer to his question. But he did know where he could find the answer. Tomorrow, he would find Haley. He would ask her if she loved him, and if the answer was yes, he…What would he do? For once he didn't know, but the thought was more exhilarating than terrifying. He would cross that bridge when it came to it. First things first, he needed to find Haley.

But that was easier said than done. Calls to her home the next day yielded nothing. When he was getting really irritated, a visitor showed up at the farm. Grant let her into Brent's office and backed out the door.

The girl stood nervously wringing her hands behind her back.

"May I help you?" Brent asked. Had she come about a job? If so, he would have to tell her the position had been filled by Haley's boyfriend, what's-his-name.

"I'm Tamara," she said, waiting to see if the name would register. Eventually it did. His face lit with a welcoming smile.

"Haley's friend. How do you do?" He stood and held out his hand over his desk. She grasped his hand and shook. "Please sit," he offered, indicating the chair beside her. She sat, still biting her lip.

"Your farm is really pretty. Haley said it was nice, but only seeing it in person can do it justice."

He smiled. "Thank you." When she didn't continue, he cleared his throat. "Have you talked to Haley lately? I've been having some trouble getting in touch with her."

She squirmed in her seat, looking miserable. "That's what I'm here to talk to you about. Um, I don't know how to say this, but Haley's gone."

He blinked at her, thinking he had misunderstood. "Gone? What do you mean she's gone?"

"I mean gone, like she packed up her stuff and left town. She told me to wait two weeks and come tell you."

"Come tell me what?" he asked, still confused.

"That she's gone."

"That's it? That's all she said?"

Tamara nodded. "And she said to give you this." She handed him a note. He ripped it open, not waiting for privacy. There were five words written on the note.

"Don't try to find me," he muttered out loud. He looked up, pinning Tamara with a gaze that made her nervous-looking face pale. "Where did she go?"

"I don't know," Tamara said. "I really don't," she added when he still looked thunderously angry. "She said if she told me, you would drag it out of me."

"Why? Why would she go?"

Tamara squirmed again. He sensed she knew the answer to that question, but then again he probably did, too. He had hurt her even more than he realized. She hadn't run away; she had run away from *him*. The knowledge brought a searing pain and he bent over.

"Um, I should go now I think," Tamara said, clearly uncomfortable. He nodded, unable to speak. Brent had never passed out before, but there was always a first time. His eyes squeezed tightly shut, waiting for the black spots to disappear. When he was feeling a little more in control, he picked up the phone. Dialing correctly took a couple of times with his quaking fingers, but he finally got the number right.

"Brent Honeywell for Mr. James," he said. Mr. James came on the line almost immediately.

"Mr. Honeywell, I was getting ready to call you. I know you said the account no longer belongs to you, that it's in the young lady's command but..." He cut off as if uncertain how to proceed.

"But what?" Brent choked.

"But she cleared it out. Every penny. It's all gone." Mr. James sounded frantic, as if he had somehow done the wrong thing. Brent should offer him some reassurances, but he had none to give. Instead he hung up the phone without saying goodbye and rested his head on his desk.

Haley was gone, and so was his heart. What was he supposed to do now?

CHAPTER 17

*S*ix months later…

Haley sat in class, her mind on anything but what the professor was saying. Outside the window, a lone mountain caught her attention. She tried to tear her eyes away and turn them back to the front of the room, but she couldn't. She had the sudden and crazy desire to skip class and climb the mountain. No doubt about it, she was losing her mind.

Montana was supposed to be a place to escape, but her problems had followed her here. Almost as soon as she arrived, she realized there was no escape for the horrible pain. There was only the hope that, with time, the ache would become duller. So far that hadn't happened. She had debated running somewhere else, but decided to stay. It was beautiful here, and the college was so cheap she could easily afford it.

Class ended and Haley gathered her books, stuffing them into her backpack. Sometimes she felt ridiculous being in college. Not only was she physically older than the other freshmen, but she felt leaps and bounds ahead of them maturity-wise, too. What did she care about partying or getting drunk? She hadn't even been into that scene in high school. While her buckled-down, no-nonsense attitude was good for her grades, it didn't do much for her social life. She said hello to a few people, but she didn't have any friends—a situation she didn't see changing anytime soon.

She dated occasionally, but none of the boys who asked her out ever measured up to the one person she couldn't have. Without exception, all of them were too young, too immature, too short, too self-involved, or any number of reasons she found for not going on a second date with any of them.

Most of the time she enjoyed her classes, but she was beginning to fear she was seeing her future stretch out before her exactly as her life was now—uneventful and alone.

She let herself into her dorm room, trying not to roll her eyes when she noticed her roommate and another girl, lying on the floor and giggling over some guy. Had she ever been that young? She didn't think so. When she was eighteen, she was trying to pay her bills and survive. Except for her biannual gifts from Brent, she hadn't had much to smile about. Now she was almost twenty one, but she felt more like fifty. Life had lost its zest. Her new goal was simply to survive, and she would do it alone.

As soon as she walked into the room, the giggles and conversation came to a halt. *That's right; the wet blanket is here. Time to stop laughing as I suck all joy from the atmosphere.* She put a mug of water in the microwave and waited for it to heat while she searched for a teabag. Slowly, conversation began to swirl again, and Haley was both relieved and annoyed by the chatter. *You could always get your own place off campus,* a little voice said. She frowned and tried to ignore it. Taking the money had been a big mistake. She had wanted the security, and she wanted to send a message to Brent, but she never intended to use it. Now whenever times got hard, it worked as a tempting reminder of how things could be different. And it was also a tempting reminder of *him,* her only tangible connection to the life she'd had before.

After her tea brewed, she dumped it in a travel mug. Once again, she would find sanctuary in the library. Even though it was April, she bundled up as if she were getting ready to face the tundra, putting on a thick parka, wool hat, mittens, and a scarf. Outside a cold gray mist was making the walkways icy, but Haley didn't care because the weather matched her mood. She was glad spring came later here. When it finally did get warm, she was afraid she would have to flee to somewhere even colder, possibly Antarctica.

The library was deserted, but why wouldn't it be? It was Friday night, after all. Only Haley and a handful of kids who were too socially awkward to have dates were present. She nodded at a couple of them, realizing as she did so that they were the Friday night regulars, and so was she.

"Pathetic," she muttered, then frantically darted her eyes to make sure no one overheard. She would hate for someone to think she was talking about him when really she was referring to herself.

She sat, becoming absorbed in her homework, when a shadow fell over her book. She looked up to see Mitch, a guy she had gone out with once a couple of months ago. Since the library wasn't his usual scene, she was surprised to see him.

"Hey, Mitch," she greeted with a smile. "Are you working on a paper?"

"No, I'm working on you, Haley." He sat in the leather chair beside her and propped his feet on the table. "You've been dodging me since we went out. At first I thought you were playing hard to get, but now I'm beginning to think you're not interested in me, and that's not possible." He grinned at her, an endearing mix of cockiness and vulnerability.

Haley returned his smile. She had originally gone out with him because he reminded her of Tyler, with his blond hair and blue eyes. She hadn't contacted Tyler since the night she and Brent had dinner with him, and she missed him. Mitch wasn't as sweet and innocent as Tyler, but he was still a nice guy.

"What can I say, Mitch? I'm not one for commitment."

"But that's what's makes it so great because neither am I. I had fun with you, and there's something about that sweet southern accent of yours that drives me a little bit crazy—in a good way. I think we should go out again. I think you want to, and you don't know it yet."

Haley looked around, putting off an answer, and as she scanned the library she once again saw her future. Why was she condemning herself to nights like these? Was she secretly still waiting for Brent to change his mind, find her, and come rescue her from her dreary existence? Since the age of five, she had looked to him as her knight in shining armor, but when she needed him most, he got off his horse and walked away. No more. Maybe she would never love anyone as much as she loved Brent, but she could still have fun.

"I want to say yes, Mitch," he smiled triumphantly until she continued, "but I have a problem."

"What problem?" he asked warily.

"Someone once told me that I'm worthy of being treated well. Last time we went out, it was nice for a first date. But you're going to have to step up your game if you want to go out again."

"You want me to spend a lot of money on you?" he asked.

"No, I want you to be creative. In fact, I don't care if you don't spend a cent. I want to know you've put some thought into it." If Brent didn't want her, at least she could take from him the lesson he had tried to teach her: she was worth more than a last-minute date when some guy had nothing better to do.

Mitch gave her a studying look. "I don't think a girl has ever asked me to step up my game before."

"Welcome to the big leagues," she said, giving him a flirtatious wink.

He laughed and stood. "Challenge accepted. I guess I'd better go think of something grand."

"Good luck," she said, causing him to chuckle as he walked away from her. She returned to her book with a smile. Maybe it wasn't Brent she loved; maybe it was the grand displays of affection. Perhaps if someone else put as much care and romance into her, she would fall for him, too. At this point, anything was worth a try.

The next Friday, Haley found herself on a date with Mitch. True to her request, he had thought up something grand. The day after their conversation in the library, she returned to her room, only to find it filled with a hundred white balloons. There was a note that said, "Will you go out with me? If the answer is yes, pop a white balloon and send it back to me. If the answer is no, pop a red balloon." Haley looked around the room and, sure enough, there were no red balloons. She popped a balloon and sent it back with a note telling him he had earned ten points for the ask-out. She also told him if he reached a hundred points, he would receive a good-night kiss.

The next day, she found a handpicked bouquet waiting outside her door. Attached was a card that read, "This is bitterroot. It's the state flower of Montana. Does that earn any extra points?"

Haley replied, telling him he had earned five points for the flowers, and five points for the trivia.

The next morning, he sent her a picture of the base of a chair, taken in such a way that it looked like a capital H. The next four mornings, she received pictures taken all over campus, and they all spelled her name—the A was the top spire of the chapel, the L was a piece of the foot bridge over the stream, the E was a piece of wrought-iron fence, and the Y was the top of a stained glass window.

On Friday evening when she answered her door, Mitch took her in his arms, and leaned in for a kiss. She shoved at his chest, taking a step back out of his embrace. "What are you doing?"

"Tell me the picture idea didn't get me to a hundred points," he said in a cocky tone she in no way found endearing. Perhaps she had created a competitive monster with her point system.

"I gave it fifty points," she said. Then, realizing how ungrateful she must sound, she softened and smiled. "And I thought it was really sweet. Thank you." She leaned up to kiss his cheek.

The cheek kiss worked to soften him, too, and he smiled. "All right, so I have thirty points left to go. I'm certain I can get there on our first stop." He took her hand and led her behind him down the hall. When they reached his car, he opened the door for her, making sure to point out that he had done so. Just when she was feeling uncertain about their upcoming evening, he seemed to mellow out, putting the point system to rest for a while. They talked about their week, and she was glad to realize she felt comfortable with him. She tried hard to stop comparing him to Brent, or even to Tyler, and to get to know him as Mitch.

Their first stop was a bowling alley.

"I love bowling," she said happily.

"We're not actually here to bowl," he said. "We're here to eat. It's two for one hot dog night." He waited expectantly to see how his announcement would be met, and then he smiled when she laughed delightedly.

"I love hot dogs," she declared. She had never actually eaten in a bowling alley before, and there was something cute about the fact that he had brought her there for the food. Especially because on their first date he had taken her to a very nice but very bland restaurant; the out-of-the-way little bowling alley showed he actually put some thought into the date.

Their pleasant conversation continued over supper. Haley thought even if romance didn't work between them, they could be friends, and that made her happy. When they finished with supper—which they had eaten on stools at a counter that looked like it hadn't been updated since the 1950's—Mitch took her to a bar. Since she wasn't into the bar scene, her heart sank until she realized it was karaoke night.

"Karaoke?" she asked, laughing.

"Singing is my secret passion, and I'm awesome at it."

As soon as he sang his first song, she realized his hyperbolic boast had been a joke because he was horrible. In fact, he was so horrible that people kept asking him to sing, merely so they could laugh at him. And he happily complied, belting out tunes with all the soul of a lounge singer. Haley was sure she hadn't laughed so much in months, but her laughter came to a halt when the announcer called her name. She looked accusingly at Mitch who shrugged.

"If you want to go out a third time, you're going to have to step up your game, Haley," he said. "Karaoke is part of the package." He shooed her toward the stage while she died twenty deaths, wondering if anyone would notice if she passed out. As a rule, she only sang in the shower. Still, Mitch was horrible and people loved him. She hoped if she was bad, she could be as bad as he was.

She selected a country song she had known since she was a little girl. Hands shaking, she took the microphone and stared at the teleprompter, following the bouncing ball as it told her when to sing. She sang softly at first, and then as she realized most of the people in the audience were too drunk to care if she was good or not, she gained confidence and began to sing louder.

When she reached the refrain, she prepared to belt it, but a tall figure stepped into the doorway, diverting her attention. She continued to sing, weakly now, only paying half attention as her eyes remained riveted on the hulking figure in the doorway. The spotlight was on her, and the doorway was dim, but there was no mistaking that figure, was there? Lots of cowboys in Montana were large, but were any that large?

In the end she became so distracted she put down the microphone and rushed off the stage, darting toward the figure. But in the few seconds it took her to sprint from the stage, he had disappeared. She reached the door and looked around, but there was no sign of the large man. Pushing open the door, she stepped out into the chill night air.

"Brent?" she said, softly at first, then louder a few times until she was almost yelling his name. When there was no answer, she closed her eyes and leaned against the side of the building, drawing deep breaths.

"Haley, are you okay?" Mitch stepped up beside her and touched her arm. She jumped and looked at him, blinking away the lingering vision of Brent's handsome face.

"I'm okay," she said, but it came out like a question. "I guess I needed some air. Maybe I'll go splash some water on my face."

Mitch gave her a hesitant smile. "Okay." They turned toward the bar and he opened the door for her. "I don't lose points for this, do I?"

She laughed and patted his stomach as she passed by him on her way to the bathroom. Once there, she wet a cloth and pressed it to the back of her neck, bending over the sink. Why was this happening to her? Why did she have to imagine Brent when she was actually out on a real date and having fun? Was she sick in the head? Did she secretly hate herself? What other explanation could there be?

"He's not real," she told herself.

"Who's not?"

Haley squealed, spun, and dropped the cloth she had been holding. Behind her stood Brent Honeywell, looking for all the world like he owned the ladies' room.

CHAPTER 18

"What are you doing here?" she blurted, backing up against the counter for support as her legs immediately went weak. Whether it was the fright at seeing him standing behind her in a mirror or her usual reaction to the sight of him, she didn't know. And she didn't care. Brent was *here*.

"I could ask you the same question," Brent said. His arms were crossed and he leaned one shoulder against the wall. His expression was neutral, but his tone was angry.

"Brent, this is the ladies' room," she said reasonably.

He made a show of looking around. "And we're the only ones here. What's the big deal?"

What was the big deal? The big deal was that she was supposed to be safe. She had come here to get away from him. She was on a *date*, for goodness sake. Since that seemed like the safest place to start, she said it out loud. "I'm on a date."

"And you're in the bathroom, bent over a sink, and trying not to cry. I'd say it's going well."

"It was going well until you showed up," she said. "I repeat my earlier 'what are you doing here?'"

"Obviously, I'm here for you."

"Wh-what?" she stammered. Was he going to drag her back to Kentucky with him?

"You packed up and left with no goodbye. I had to make sure you're okay; I had to make sure you're doing well."

"I'm okay," she said shakily. "I'm doing well." She sounded unconvincing, even to her own ears.

"I'm not sure about that," he said, narrowing his eyes at her. "You look pale."

"There's not much sun in Montana this time of year."

"You look thinner," he added.

"You're starting to sound like my mother," she said, frowning.

"Have you talked to your mother since you've been here?" he asked.

"No," she said, twisting the hem of her shirt uncomfortably.

"So you took off, running halfway across the country without a word of your whereabouts to anyone." He made a tsking noise and shook his head. "And I thought you were mature, Haley."

Some of Haley's fiery temper returned to her then. She strode forward and poked his chest, hard, although of course only her finger was hurt by the action. "Don't call me immature. You wrote the book on being immature."

He didn't respond, but his eyes kindled with something intense, something that frightened her so that she dropped her hand and took a step back.

"How did you find me?" she muttered.

"A very expensive team of private detectives," he said.

She frowned again. "I told you not to; I told you not to look for me."

"So you did," he said evenly. "You're finally in college, I see."

She nodded, fastening onto that piece of information like a lifeline. "That's right. I'm in college, like you wanted. I'm settled here, and Montana is beautiful. I'm doing okay. You can go home now and forget you ever saw me."

There was a long pause. He caught her eyes and held them, pinning her with his intense gaze. "Is that what you want?"

"It doesn't matter what I want," she said. "It's never mattered to you."

His expression remained poker-faced neutral, but his eyes seethed with anger, causing her to shiver. "How's the money holding out?" he asked. "Need any more?"

Now it was her turn for her eyes to snap with fury. "I don't need or want your money. I haven't touched a dime from that account, and if you took every penny today, I'd be happy to never see it again. In fact, I wish you would."

For the first time, his cool expression slipped, revealing astonishment. "You didn't use the money?"

She shook her head fervently.

"You moved halfway across the country to go to college, and you didn't tap your college fund?" he asked. His voice was a mixture of incredulity and something else she couldn't comprehend.

"The money isn't mine to use," she said. "I withdrew it from the account, that's true, but I never intended to use it. I put it in a high-interest account, so I think I actually made a little bit for you. I intended to return it to you after I finished college. I thought if you thought I was using it, you wouldn't look for me."

"You thought wrong," he said slowly. He eased off the wall and she froze, waiting for him to advance, waiting for him to say something, waiting for anything other than the unbearable silence that was now suspended between them. At last he straightened, seemingly having arrived at an internal decision.

"Well, I can see you're doing well here. I'll go now. Have fun on your date." He smiled, turned, and then he was gone.

Haley stood staring mutely at the door. That was it? He had spent six months tracking her down, and that was it? That was all he was going to do about her absence? She ran after him, seething, but when she burst through the double set of outside doors, he was no longer in sight.

"How does he do that?" she said, kicking angrily at a rock in her path. Reluctantly, she turned and went back inside, but the remainder of the date was ruined. She tried to put up a good front for Mitch, but he saw through her ruse and offered to take her home. Fortunately, he blamed her now-frazzled state on illness. But his care and concern made the knife of guilt twist that much deeper. That was why, when they reached her dorm room, she surprised him by turning to practically throw herself at him, kissing him senseless.

He clung to her and would have kissed her again, but she was already regretting her hasty decision to kiss him in the first place. She withdrew, smiling gently at his dazed face.

"I guess I reached a hundred points," he said, sounding mildly confused by her mixed signals.

"You reached a thousand," she told him. "Tonight was great. This whole week was great. You went over and above all my expectations."

He frowned. "Why do I sense a but in there somewhere?"

Her smile turned sad. "But I'm in no shape to date right now. I'm sorry. My life is confusing, and..." she would have continued, but the door she was leaning on—her door—suddenly opened and she fell inside, or she would have if Brent hadn't caught her.

"Well, about time you two got home. How was the date?" He smiled and looked between them.

Mitch froze, looking confused and a little frightened of Brent's hulking size. "Is this your dad?" he asked Haley. Haley winced, but Brent laughed.

She swallowed. "No, uh, Brent is my...he's my..."

"What is the end of that sentence, Haley?" Brent asked innocently. He and Mitch both stood waiting for her to answer, staring at her from opposite sides.

"F-friend?" she stammered.

Brent shook his head. "Friends don't go off half cocked across the country, not even saying goodbye." He rested his hands on the top of the doorframe, leaning out so he towered over her, a couple of inches away. "Do they?"

"Um, maybe I should go," Mitch said, sounding uncomfortable.

Haley swiveled to look at him with an apologetic look. "I'm so sorry," she said. "I had no idea he was going to be here." She would have said more, but Brent was loudly drumming his fingers on the doorframe, drowning out most of the conversation.

"It's okay," Mitch said, but his grimace told her it was anything but okay. He turned and darted away.

"Scared little rabbit, isn't he?' Brent asked as he watched Mitch's retreating backside.

Haley turned and shoved at his chest until he backed up into her room, then she entered the room and slammed her door. She stood on her toes, trying to see around Brent to make sure her roommate wasn't in the room. When she was certain they were alone, she unleashed her fury on him.

"What do you think you're doing? You have no right to barge into my room and interrupt my date, a date that was going very well until you showed up, thank you very much."

He grinned and plopped on her bed, making it groan under his weight. "You're welcome," he said sincerely.

She fisted her hands on her hips, glaring at him. "Brent, what are you doing?"

His grin didn't waver. "Did I ever tell you you're pretty when you're angry?"

"Stop, stop right there," she said. She moved her hands to her temples and pressed, trying to ward off her budding headache. "We are not going down this road again. This isn't Kentucky; this is Montana. I'm not your ward or whatever you deluded yourself into thinking I am. I'm a grown woman, and you can't manhandle my life." She opened her eyes and focused hard on his face. "I want you to go, and I want you to go right now."

Slowly, he shook his head.

Haley stamped her foot in frustration. "What do you mean no? I can call the campus police and have you thrown out, you know."

He gave her a slow smile. "You think so, sugar? How many of them are there?"

He had her there, and he knew it; it would probably take an army to make a Honeywell do something he didn't want to do. She was on the verge of a full-tilt meltdown. She had to get rid of him before that happened.

"Why are you doing this?" she asked weakly.

"Because you didn't use the money," he said.

She blinked at him, confused. "What?"

"The money," he repeated. "I finally figured out why you wouldn't use it."

"Why?" she asked uncertainly, not at all sure she wanted him to answer.

"Because you love me," he said matter-of-factly.

"What?" Her hand flew nervously to her throat. Had someone told? The only people who knew were Coy and Ivy, but they wouldn't betray her confidence, would they? "How did you arrive at that conclusion?"

He smiled wider because she hadn't denied it. "I've had six lonely, miserable months to think about a lot of things, and I came to some realizations about you. The first is that you're in love with me."

"Did you have any realizations about yourself?" she asked, peeved.

He nodded. "But we're talking about you now. I realized that the reason you don't want to use the money is because you don't want to be beholden to me."

"I don't want to be beholden to anyone," she said.

"True, but especially not to me. It galls you to think of me as your benefactor, to think of me as the man who paid your way to college. But, guess what, sugar, I *am* going to pay your way to college."

She shook her head, but he wouldn't allow her to speak. He stood and advanced on her. "Know what else I realized about you?" he asked. She was still shaking her head, and he took that as encouragement. "I realized you're not a little girl anymore. You're a full-grown woman." He reached her and rested his hands on her waist, jerking her close so that she was pressed against his chest.

"I'm ready to hear some realizations about you now," she said nervously. She had never seen such an intense glint in his eyes before tonight, and it was making her uneasy. He looked almost wild.

"We'll get to me in a minute," he said.

Once again, her temper boiled over. "No." She tried to wriggle away from him, but he wouldn't let her. "I'm tired of talking about me, Brent; it's all we ever do. So I love you, big deal. You can't tell me you haven't always known. You want to know something about you? You like to pretend you're too old for me, but you're not. Physically you may be thirty two, but you have the maturity of a fifteen-year-old. And you know what else?"

He shook his head, smiling amusedly at her.

"You have ruined me for other men," she declared.

He hadn't been expecting that, and his smile vanished. "What are you talking about? What other men?"

"The other men I've tried to date since I went away. If you didn't want me, then why did you treat me so well no one else could ever measure up?" Tonight with Mitch had been the best date she'd had, and it still hadn't measured up to her most mundane times with Brent.

"Are you finished?" he asked.

"For now," she said, trying to maintain her pride and keep her tears at bay. She could feel them, hovering not far away. Why did he have to find her if he still didn't want her? Why, why, why?

His hands clamped on her biceps and squeezed. Her first thought was that he must not realize how tightly he was gripping her because he would never hurt her, even in a fit of temper.

"Okay, now it's my turn. Listen up, honey, because I'm only going to say this once. You're right. I was wrong about everything, and I'm sorry."

Her lashes fluttered in surprise. "What?" Haley was almost certain he had never said the words "I was wrong" before. Previously she had assumed such an admission wasn't even in his vocabulary. She shook her arms, trying to loosen his vice-like grip on her. Her reminder worked and he let go her arms, smoothing his hands down to her hips.

"Since the day we met, I've always wanted to do what's best for you. It never occurred to me that what's best for you might be me. And until you went away, I didn't know I loved you. I've never been in love before. I had no idea it was supposed to be terrifying."

"You love me?" She said the words slowly, wonderingly, questioningly.

"I'd better. I spent a year's salary trying to find you." He picked her up so they were eye level. "Of course I love you, Haley, and I want to be with you, if you want to be with an old broken down jalopy like me."

In answer, she kissed him, and he didn't seem to mind at all that she made the first move. In fact, if his response was any indication, he rather enjoyed it.

"There's one more thing," he said when the long kiss was finished.

"What?"

"You're going to finish college before we have kids."

"We'll see," she said. "I'm not making any promises." She pulled him close, kissing him again.

"We'll see," he agreed sometime later, and she smiled, knowing she had won.

They were married three months later. Haley at first protested the quick engagement, telling Brent there was no way she could pull together a wedding in such a short amount of time, and certainly not a fashionable society wedding like one befitting the Honeywells. She realized her mistake as soon as she saw the challenging glint in Brent's eyes.

"Oh, we can do it," he assured her. She should have realized that "we" included not only the two of them, but all four of his brothers and Ivy, as well. Ivy was put in charge of helping Haley find her dress and bridesmaids' dresses, and the men took care of everything else. Occasionally Brent would ask her opinion on music or flowers, but, by and large, he did everything on his own, including address the invitations. She would never forget the night she had walked into the den to see all five brothers writing in calligraphy, a stack of invitations and addresses beside them.

And she would never forget the look on the pastor's face when the brothers deemed the chapel unsuitable for a wedding. They had renovated it, creating a center aisle and building a gazebo for her and Brent to stand under while they said their vows. She supposed most women would protest at having their future husband and his brothers as their wedding planners, but Haley didn't really care. She had never been into party-planning, and she was so happy to be back in Kentucky and engaged to Brent that they could have told her she was getting married on a trash heap and she would have happily agreed.

Brent, on the other hand, became so exacting that Haley called him a groomzilla. After three caterers quit, she decided to step in and run interference, acting as the buffer between the unwitting caterer and her detail-loving fiancé.

The wedding preparations were having an unexpected effect on Haley's mother, too. At first when she called Haley and asked to have lunch, Haley was suspicious. Had Steve sensed a windfall and put her mother up to it? But, no, Steve hadn't been mentioned. And, miracle of miracles, her mother finally explained a little of her uncaring attitude.

"I've never been one much for children, Haley. I guess it's no secret that I didn't want them. Your father sort of tricked me into it." Haley's heart felt lanced until she continued. "But you're not a child anymore; you're a lovely woman, and I would like to get to know you a little better. I know I haven't always been the most attentive mother." She paused to give Haley a sheepish smile. "I can't promise you that's going to change completely, but I would like to be friends, if we can."

It wasn't the glowing declaration of love Haley had craved all her life, but it was a start. Maybe it was time for Haley to stop trying to fit her mother into a mold she had created and accept her for who she was and what she could give--a decision that was made easier by Haley's blooming relationship with Brent's mother. In her, she found all the maternal devotion she had always longed for. Despite the fact that she had six children, she still had an abundance of love to share. Together, she and Mrs. Honeywell jumped into wedding planning, at least as much as the brothers and Brent would allow.

If Haley had any doubts about letting the Honeywell men plan her wedding, they were erased when she caught sight of the sanctuary early on the morning of her wedding. It was beautiful. Not only had they created the center aisle, and added a gazebo, but they had also replaced the windows with stained glass in order to appease the pastor and church members who were upset at the renovations. The colored glass caught the light, causing fractures of rainbows to bounce around the room. There were so many flowers and plants, Haley was reminded of an arboretum, and there were also hundreds upon hundreds of tiny white lights. They even covered the ceiling, draped in tulle to resemble a hazy dream, though she had no idea how they were held aloft.

"Do you like it?" Brent asked.

She jumped and spun, ducking behind a door. "You're not supposed to see me," she said.

"My eyes are closed," he said. "I felt my way along the wall."

She poked her head out and, indeed, his eyes were pinched tightly closed.

"Does the superstition say anything about being able to hold you?" he asked, holding out his arms in the totally wrong direction so he was facing the wall.

She smiled and eased forward, spinning him around and stepping into his embrace. He buried his face her in neck and she stood on her toes, trying to get as close to him as possible.

"Guess what?" he said.

"Hmm," she said, smiling in utter contentment.

"I decided to let you choose your present today. What do you want?"

She almost said she only wanted him. Who cared about anything else? Although, there was one thing she cared about, something she wanted more than anything. "I want a three month old this time next year," she said.

His grip tightened on her waist. "And everyone thinks I'm the relentless one in our relationship. What about college?"

"I don't want to go to college. I want to have babies, lots and lots of babies."

"You're turning feminism on its ear, you know that?" he said, though he was smiling.

She nodded.

He sighed. "Promise me something."

"Anything."

"Promise me that, if someday you feel restless, like you need or want more, promise me you'll go to college, no matter how old you are."

"I promise," she said. "After all, age is only a number, right?"

"Keep telling yourself that," he said. He kissed her shoulder, and she shivered. "What if I give you something better than a baby?"

She frowned. "What could be better than a baby?" she asked.

"Two babies," he said. "Did I ever tell you that twins run in the Honeywell family?"

She smiled. "And you think you can give me twins because you decide to?"

"Sweetheart, you're about to become a Honeywell. That means you need to start thinking like one. If you want something, you go for it, and it's yours. That's the way it works." He gave her a squeeze. "That's the way it worked with you."

"Okay," she agreed. "Next year by this time I want two babies," she declared.

"And I will do my level best to give them to you," he said gravely, making her laugh again.

A year later, when she only had one baby, she arched an accusing eyebrow at him over the top of their daughter's head. "I thought you promised me twins."

"Did I say twins?" he asked, backpedaling. "I meant Irish twins like me and Corliss. We're only ten months apart, you know."

Haley laughed, wincing when the effort hurt. "That wasn't what I meant, and I really don't see that happening." She grimaced as she shifted positions.

Brent took the baby from her, leaning forward to kiss her. "We'll see," he said. And they did, ten months later when their second baby girl was born.

. . .

Thank you for reading *Wild Stallions,* The first book in the Honeywells of Kentucky series. For more books, please check out my website at www.vanessagraybartal.com